YA FI
Krova~~~, ~~~~~~pher.
Heavy metal and you

Heavy Metal
and You

GO THERE.

OTHER TITLES AVAILABLE FROM PUSH

Heavy Metal
and You

Christopher Krovatin

PUSH

SCHOLASTIC INC.

NEW YORK TORONTO LONDON AUCKLAND SYDNEY

MEXICO CITY NEW DELHI HONG KONG BUENOS AIRES

ISBN 0-439-73648-X

Library of Congress Cataloging-in-Publication Data
Available

12 11 10 9 8 7 6 5 4 3 2   5 6 7 8 9 10/0

Printed in the U.S.A.   40
First printing, June 2005

*This book is dedicated
to Emily Boyd
and Alex Wenner,
who love me
none the less.*

Acknowledgments

I have to begin by thanking my incredible family for always being there for me, no matter how many Cannibal Corpse songs I played on the car stereo. Mom, Dad, Quin, Maria — you have enlightened and enhanced me with your respective presences, and I can't thank you enough for it. Someday I will repay you.

Next, I have to thank all of my friends who have stood by me and helped me out. There are too many to name you all individually, but you know who you are and everything you've ever done for me. I send my love to all my boys from Collegiate, all my friends at Wesleyan, all my siblings in the Phi, and everyone in between. Most of all, though, I'd like to thank James McBride and Nick Altman, two young men who've made me the crass, annoying, paranoid, insecure, psychotic creature that you see on the back of this book. Gentleman, I owe you more than I could ever say. You are my safety net; my life is yours.

Thanks must also be rained down on David Levithan, my incredible editor and friend, and everyone at Scholastic. David, you have trusted and believed in me through all of this, which is more than I can say about most. You are a brilliant writer, a spectacular friend, and overall one of the better people I can think of. Without you, I wouldn't be here. I can't begin to thank you enough. Anica, Billy, Nico, Jeff, Josh, Thu: thank you for the same. At a time when I considered myself expendable, you all reminded me that I was of some worth.

In all seriousness, I send my deepest love to any and every girl who has been sweet and stupid enough to care for me. As much of a basket case as I was and still am, your kindness and nurturing have given me an understanding of the world and how it should be seen. I don't deserve the gifts you've given me through your grace, and I can only hope that you'll one day know how much I appreciate it.

And finally, I'd like to thank all of the musicians who have inspired me over the years. When the world was using me for a punching bag and life had no meaning whatsoever, I could find healing, strength, and peace through throwing one of your CDs on the stereo and fronting the bands in my bathroom mirror.

Special thanks to Tom, Jeff, Dave, and Paul, for being Slayer.

Right before this book went to press, one of heavy metal's champions was taken from us. In a world that makes itself out to be invincible, it is horrible to see that ignorance and idiocy can harm us in such a way. Metal will always be about those things that drive us — the objects, feelings, and causes that make us wake up every morning with our fists clenched in determination. Those who forget that drape a shroud of sadness and anger over us all. We miss you, Darrel. But we will keep on walking.

chapter 1
Sabra Cadabra

▷

"I'm afraid I'm going to start blathering in a couple seconds."

She gazed at me with that chin-up, down-her-face look and said, "I like it when you blather."

"You're wonderful," I blathered, throwing my hands down and avoiding her stare. "You're just great. And I'm really nervous, and you've just been great, and I'm so sure I've blown tonight completely. And I'm sorry. And you're funny, and you're gorgeous, and I'm just so fucking amazed right now at how great you are. And I'm going to lose you."

She did this thing where she leaned her weight onto one leg and kind of slouched, throwing her head back at a diagonal so that she was looking right down her face at me. It was like I was an Eight-ball and she was sizing me up for the crack. She'd been doing it all night, and it was driving me nuts. She was sexy — not in an oversexed, flaunting-it way, but in a cute, waiting-to-be-taken way. She was wearing an old blue nurse's uniform that she'd probably found at a Salvation Army store. That and the white garter-belt stockings were not helping. I was completely drawn in.

A smile crept across her perfect, wonderful lips. She slumped forward a little, shaking her head, breaking into a grin. Then she walked slowly over to me, threw her arms around my neck, and kissed me. It was perfect. I mean, absolutely perfect. Those full, rounded lips grasping mine. Tongue, but not too much: a flicker of hers, a split second of that soft, porous touch. We stood in the light of a Central Park streetlamp and kissed, softly and carefully, both of us nervous as hell. (Or maybe it was just me. . . .) My hands found their way around her waist, and I pulled her to me, her stomach against mine, her breasts pressing against my overcoat. This was what I wanted from the night. She was what I'd been looking for.

I pulled my head back a little and whispered, "Um, okay."

She cut me off with another kiss.

◁◁

She'd shown up exactly on time. The smoky little café I'd picked had fancy-looking food and attractive waiters in clean uniforms, but also had wooden tables with writing scratched into them and old black-and-white movie posters on the walls. I thought it suited her. I'd been keeping the name in my head so that when I finally got the courage up to ask her out at play rehearsal, it would seem like I had at least some sort of taste or culture or brain.

I'd spent all afternoon going over how awkward this was going to be, the dark and stormy actor and the chipper lighting girl stuck in a stuffy little room with nothing to say to each other. The outfit had floored me. She obviously knew how to impress a guy like me, and that made me so happy I'd wanted to scream. But it was her, it was her hair, it was the sort of halo she seemed to give off. I . . . wanted. I wanted so badly.

She'd walked over, sat down, and chirped, "Hey."

"Hey. How was your day?"

She smiled. "Good!"

"What'd you do?"

"Looked forward to this."

Wham. I swallowed what felt like a ball of light. "Oh."

"What about you?"

"Um, y'know, about the same."

She laughed. "Good."

Talk slowly turned small, with us throwing back and forth witty commentary about school and idiot banter about everything else. It became obvious that we were both freaking out just a wee bit, and the massive mugs of highly caffeinated mud we were slurping down weren't helping in the least. Finally, after a mug and a biscotti each, I looked up to ask what she wanted to do, and found she was staring at me down her face. I managed to ask her why she was staring at me, and her mouth curled up at the corners like the Grinch when he got a wonderful, awful idea. We just stared at each other for about fifteen minutes, and even when the waitress asked us if we wanted the check, I managed to pay for the whole thing without once breaking my gaze from hers.

Finally: "Okay, really, what're you looking at?"

"You."

". . . I'm a little nervous."

"Yeah."

A pause.

"Let's go for a walk through the park, okay?"

"I was hoping you'd say that."

▷

We must've spent at least half an hour standing there in each other's arms, just making out in the park. The cold didn't really matter. Neither did the condescending glances from the strangers passing by. One guy even had the gall to mutter "Get a room" under his breath. Any other circumstances, I would've gone running after him with my middle finger raised. But I didn't. I just held her and kissed her and was momentarily content.

Finally, I killed the mood by pulling back and saying that I had to get home early. She yanked me towards the street and we spilled out onto Central Park West, heading across town towards my house, stopping occasionally for a kiss or two or several more. We were generally silent, maybe a word or two passing between us. We didn't need to say anything. We were fine as it was.

She dropped me off across the street from my place around eleven-thirty. I held her close and kissed her one last time before running to catch the light. I wanted to dance, sing, throw my arms in the air, and fly away on the cold night sky. She was great. I'd made a catch. Hell, I'd made *the* catch! I was a friggin' god.

4

I unlocked my front door and skipped up the stairs into my foyer, humming a Morbid Angel tune under my breath. My family lived in a brownstone house on the Upper West Side. My folks made quite a bit of money, so my brother, sister, and I were always provided for. We were fortunate, well-raised kids. And I was a friggin' god, apparently.

Before retiring for the evening, I kissed my mom good night and told Erica, my sister, to turn down her damn bubblegum pop. The night had been perfect. Perfect. But it was missing something. Flicking through the pages of my CD binder, I found what I craved so badly: a little Celtic Frost, maybe some Misfits, and a lot of Type O Negative. I pushed *Morbid Tales*, *Famous Monsters*, and *Bloody Kisses* into my stereo and pressed PLAY.

◁◁

I was in the car with my family, driving to some family function. One of my uncles was getting married or something, and it seemed like a garish waste of my precious time. I was somewhere between eight and ten, and my older brother was discovering this crazy thing called rock and roll, constantly gabbing about some bald idiot named Billy Corgan. While we waited for our dad to finish paying for the unleaded, Carver leaned forward and turned on the radio.

Oh my God, I thought, listening to the sounds blasting from our car. *Oh my God, what is THIS?*

A wall of electronic sound came rushing out, washing over me with so much atmosphere and *power* that my preteen mind was blown away. My eyes went wide and I asked my mom to turn it up even more, fascinated by the voice coming out of the speakers on my side.

This was insane! There was some lunatic on the radio screaming something at the top of his lungs about a head being like a hole, and something else about bowing down and getting what you deserve! What did that mean? What was this guy singing about? Was he even really singing? Was it even a "he"? And what God-forsaken instruments created the beautiful noise backing him up? The car stereo immediately became Linda Blair in *The Exorcist* to me: frightening, enthralling, and undoubtedly cool.

"Yeah, Nine Inch Nails are okay," sighed Carver, slumping back in his seat, "but not as good as the Pumpkins." I didn't listen. I was so enraptured by the musical darkness filling me, a noise that at the time seemed like the sounds of a war against all things good, the soundtrack to a temple being burned to the ground.

🔲🔲

My music was my goddam life, or most of it, anyway. Honest. My life had a soundtrack at all times, and that soundtrack was one hundred percent grade-A METAL. Sure, I listened to lots of different music — a little punk, a little pop, even a little country — but metal was everything to me. At any hour in which I could get away with it, I was blasting Exodus on my stereo or slamming my head to Dimmu Borgir with my headphones on. My teeth were nice commodities, and I did enjoy having kidneys, but I'd give them all away if someone threatened to take my Slayer albums from me. Heavy metal is like that — your music defines you to the point where you need it. You don't own an article of clothing without a band logo on it, and your room is plastered with posters of your favorite bands because you need all of that fed into you. I was heavy metal. It mattered to me more than anything.

Well, then there was this girl. Melissa. This goddess I'd just left. She mattered, too.

▷

I flopped down on my beanbag chair and listened. Sure enough, a chorus of harmonized screams flooded out of my speakers, followed by a round of cult necrothrash. Celtic Frost, *Morbid Tales*. Excellent album: dark, melodic thrash with enough sheer unholiness to snap your puny head off your neck. I nestled my head into the beanbag and let the music wash over me.

She was fucking amazing. She was beautiful and wonderful and I was a god.

"INTO THE CRYPT OF RAYS!"

Tonight was perfect. *Christ*, she was incredible . . .

"INTO THE CRYPT OF RAYS!"

The night had to be ended right then, I decided. On a good note. I picked my body up, dragging it to the bathroom, getting it undressed, and finally plopping it down onto my bed. Sleep was quick to approach: it'd been a long week, and a great Saturday night. Rest was in order. I flicked my stereo remote,

7

shutting the music down in the middle of "Procreation of the Wicked." My eyes went heavy, and my mind began to wander.

She's great. She's everything I've wanted for a long time. Her tongue, and her face, and . . . those eyes . . . and . . .

I passed out, tired, with Frost lyrics and a wonderful girl rushing across my frontal lobes.

chapter 2
Wasted Youth Crew

Normally, I just nodded to the doorman of my school, an all-boys prep school that was supposed to turn me into an upstanding young man. (I know, I find it funny, too.) That Monday, I showed him a huge ear-to-ear smirk and gave him a cowboy shot with my fingers. He chuckled and shook his head, giving me a sentence or two of silence. The mouth moved, but nothing reached my ears other than Max Cavalera's voice. Sepultura was a sign of a good day — only on a good day could I actually start off with brutal Brazilian death metal. I stomped down the halls happily, straightening my tie. (Dress code. Didn't mind all that much.)

"NO CONFORMITY IN MY INNER SELF! ONLY I GUIDE MY INNER SELF!" Dunna-da-dunna-da-dunna-da-dunna-da-(was I becoming a *Beavis & Butt-Head* character?) dunna-da-dun —

A huge weight slammed onto my back, and I went stumbling forward, my arms swinging in windmills like I was a tightrope walker about to meet the safety net face-first. I listened to the long, resounding *EEEEEEP* of my Discman as I pressed the STOP button, and whipped around.

Brent stood in his usual uniform: blacks and grays, extremely preppy. Black leather shoes, gray Armani shirt, black tie, black shades, gray slacks, black leather jacket (not the biker kind, the Donna Karan kind). His face surrounded a huge smile, hair tumbling from his head like the Red Sea turned black and gelled. John, or Irish, as we called him, was on the ground next to him (seeing as I'd just thrown the boy from my back). He chuckled, a bright-red curl falling in front of his forehead. Usual outfit as well: vintage-store jacket, punkish-looking collared shirt, red tie, torn jeans, Airwalks. I, of course, was in my oh-so-trendy outfit: jeans, Doc Marten combats, black overcoat, shirt, tie, spiked wristbands, headphones, and acne.

"Conan the Barbarian," laughed Brent as Irish pulled himself up, "what do you have first period?"

"Um, gym." This was a game of ours.

"I'm sorry . . . what class?"

"Gym. P.E. Phys ed. Running with Coach Sadist."

"One more time?"

"Going-out-and-having-a-cigarette-with-you-guys class?"

"Really?" said Irish with mock excitement. "Oh my God! Me and Brent have that class, too!"

We sauntered out, laughing, talking about stupid things like the weekend homework and how much we hated school. I winked at the doorman on the way out, shooting him a thumbs-up.

"You're an insensitive idiot. Holden Caulfield is one of the most complex and important characters in modern literature and blowing him off as a 'whiny little bitch' just proves your ignorance, not his lack of relevance. You're entitled to your opinion, man, but it's my opinion that you should be taken out back and beaten with a hose."

I forget whether the guy was a wrestler or a football player. Whichever he was, all that mattered was him jumping over his desk at me and yelling, "You wanna go, new kid? You wanna go?" Two of his jock friends grabbed him and held him back, making sure to shoot me dirty looks as they sat him down and cooled him off. The teacher yelled at us all to be quiet, but not before one of them decided to shout "Fucking QUEER." Great. I'd left my last school thinking a change of scenery for high school would show me a new world, that I could get away from all the stupidity. So far, everyone seemed the same.

When English class ended, I took my time packing up my backpack. I wanted to be the last one out; hopefully, Chongo and his buddies would have disappeared by the time I left the room. When I finally looked up at the door, I didn't see them. Instead, I saw a stringy-haired kid dressed all in black, the one who always sat across from me in history. He leaned casually against the door frame with a lazy smirk on his face. Behind his hair shone bright, devilish eyes.

"Sam, right?"

I nodded, my shoulders rising.

"That was ballsy, kid," he said, shaking his head.

"Sorry. I mean . . . whatever. He pissed me off with that, y'know?"

His hand shot out. "Brent Bolmen. Pleased to meet you. I like the spiked bracelets, by the way."

I smiled. A little. "Thanks."

"You doing anything for lunch yet?"

"Uh, no. Not really."

He shot me a smile I liked from the minute I saw it. He motioned towards the door, and we walked out together.

▷

"So, guys, how was *your* Saturday night?"

Irish glanced at Brent apprehensively. "Did you tell him? *I* wanted to tell him."

"Nah, go ahead."

Irish grinned at me, his punky red hair making him look like a madman. "So, guess what we did."

Childish laughter rose in my throat. "Mmmm, got drunk?"

"FUCK YES WE GOT DRUNK!" The laughs burst from all three of us, pouring out of our throats. "I imbibed enough whiskey to kill a large ape and then puked an entire calzone into Jamie's shoe!" Our disgust led to more laughter, and soon we were helping each other stand up. It was like that with Irish and Brent. I trusted them more than anyone in the world. From day one, they'd never judged me or treated me as an outsider in any way. They ragged on me, sure, but we all did that. Our way of saying "You matter to me" was to say "I did your mom."

"Choice, guys, very choice. I wish I'd been there." I did, too.

Whenever my friends had a good time and I wasn't there, I felt cheated.

Then Brent caught on, and it began.

"You're happy today. That's not on the itinerary."

"Beg your pardon?"

He shrugged. "You're not normally happy. You're normally tired or depressed or angry or devious or . . . hungry. But not usually happy. What's up?"

"Hungry isn't an emotion, you moron."

"Enough. Talk."

"I don't know." I sighed. "I'm just in a good mood, is all."

"Ah," said Brent slyly. "You got mad amounts of play from this new girl."

"There's a new girl?" Irish jumped in. "What's the deal? Pleeeeease someone tell me the deal!"

"Sam has a new woman. S'pimping it hardcore."

"What?" Irish asked suspiciously. "Which chick is this? Where does she go to school?"

"If word on the grapevine is right, it's that girl Melissa. You've seen her in the halls, probably, after school when the girls from the play are here. She's doing lighting."

Irish shook his head. "You know I don't do the theater thing. What does she look like?"

"Long brown hair, really curvy, a very skinny neck. Blue nail polish."

"*That* girl?! Sam bagged THAT girl?!" Irish yelled, looking at me. I turned pink. "How does that *happen*? I'm better-looking than you! I'm cooler than you! I'm smarter and thinner than you!"

"I have a bigger penis, is all," I said, shrugging. Irish snarled and checked me into a parked car. Laughter, cigarette flicking, and vulgar insults ran all around. As Irish ended a rant on the truly scandalous things he was going to do with a pitchfork and some K-Y jelly, Brent put his arm on my shoulder.

"She, uh . . . she wash your salami?"

"Jesus, man," I said. "That's uncalled for."

"That's a yes if I've ever heard one."

"It is not! I've been with her ONCE! That's IT!"

"Hey, Irish! Is being with a girl once enough time to get your salami washed?"

"Your **mom** certainly thinks so."

"I hate you guys. I swear to God, I'm gonna get new friends."

"Hah!" Irish laughed, pointing at me. "Sam hangs out with losers! His friends suck! He — wait. Fuck you, too."

"Brent couldn't make it."

I looked up from my plate of steak and eggs. In front of me stood a ragged, red-haired punk in vintage clothes from head to toe, staring at me with a completely impartial look: I could either be someone new and cool or a pesky insect in need of destroying.

I frowned. "Oh. Um, okay. Who're you?"

"John McKinney. Call me Irish. Everyone does." He glanced at the seat next to me, then to my shirt. "GWAR, huh? Never much of a metal fan myself . . . you're new here, right?"

"Yeah. I just started going here."

"Any reason? Were you thrown out?"

I felt like I was being interrogated. "No, I just got really fucking bored with my old school. I'm Sam, by the way."

"Yeah, I know. Brent sent me to apologize for him and all that, and told me I should have breakfast with you and all."

"You're friends with Brent?"

"Yeah. Outside of school and all, we hang out. Party. Debauch. You know, the usual."

I nodded, forking eggs together. "He's been urging me to come out one of these nights. I might join you."

"You should. It's pretty nuts."

Irish slid into the seat across from me. After a few seconds, he said softly, "Hey, you know what's the most horrible thing ever?"

"What?" I asked, shoveling a large pile of scrambled eggs into my mouth.

He grinned. "Finding blood in your stool!"

Eggs fucking everywhere. We were friends from then on.

We sat down on our stoop around the corner, sighing from fatigue. I wondered about the trouble I was going to get in for cutting gym, but my daydreams elbowed out my worries, filtering back to her, to her body and her voice and her smile and the way her hair smelled, until I looked over and saw Brent staring at me, expecting a response.

"Sorry, what?"

"Did you do the history paper this weekend, or were you too busy getting your game on?"

"Um, yeah, it's all done. And enough of the dirty talk, kid."

"Wow . . . did you do the homework *while* getting your rocks off?"

"Irish, man! What the — well, actually, that would be pretty great."

Brent pulled out a second cigarette, lighting it expertly. I smoked, yeah, and so did Irish, but Brent, man, he sucked 'em down like no other. Maybe he had some sort of major oral fixation, or maybe he had terrible ADD and needed to self-medicate. But I don't think that was really it. What it came down to was, Brent loved smoking. It was an activity for all of us: We smoked because we liked doing it, not because we were addicted. Brent, though, he made it his *thing*. Some people made model cars. Some people played football. I acted and listened to heavy metal. Brent smoked.

"I cannot believe," he said, spouting little puffs of tobacco, "that you're allowed to hand that fucking thing in as an academic assignment. I'd *kill* to do that paper."

"Really? Why?"

"Why? Because you wrote a paper about *voodoo*, man! I mean, that's a dream paper for a freaky-ass metal boy like yourself."

"It was still a lot of work, y'know."

"Yeah, but, dude, I bet you loved every minute of it," Irish said. I shrugged. It had been pretty damn fun. History papers were not my biggest talent, but this one had been a cinch. Zombies, werewolves, magic, dark gods, foreign lands — stuff I'd have studied on my own time. Brent had spent the entire weekend bitching about having to write on trading routes, and his jealousy had only fueled my love for the paper. I had one up on Brent? Life was pretty damn good right then.

I suddenly realized I was staring off into space. Irish noticed it, too, and decided to add some commentary.

"Dude, if you're gonna fantasize about the insane amounts of hot, sweaty action you got this weekend, do it on your own goddam time."

"Yeah," Brent chimed in, that sinful little smile blossoming again. "The last thing we need is your ass daydreaming about it all when you could be describing it to us."

"I swear to God, I'm getting new friends," I mumbled. I'd said that almost every day I'd hung out with them for the past three years.

Brent grinned at me, rubbing my head. "Our big, spiky Conan. We know you love us."

He finished his smoke and we walked slowly back towards school.

chapter 3
Hallowed Be Thy Name

▷

Her phone rang a third time and I prayed for the machine.

"Hello?"

Shit. "Hey, Melissa?"

"Mmm-hmm?"

"It's Sam."

"Sam?"

"Sammy Markus? From the play? We went on that date —"

"Oh, Sammy! Hey, sorry, don't worry, I know who you are!"

Whew. "So, um, I was just thinking that maybe —"

"Do you believe in Santa, Sam?"

". . . Sorry?"

"Santa Claus. Do you believe in him?"

Oh my fucking *God*. The little voice went off in the back of my mind: This was a deciding question. I had to figure out what the perfect answer to this question would be. If I said I didn't believe in Santa, she'd think I didn't have enough of the ethereal in me, that I wasn't magical enough. If I said I did, I'd obviously be lying, and that might not seem too good, either. I had to think up an answer that encompassed both, that let in my personality while at the same time was witty or ironic or . . . whatever. The point was, this was hardly the time to screw up.

Santa Claus. Christ, but that was a good one.

I finally chose honesty.

"I'd like to," I said.

She laughed. "Good answer!"

I wiped the invisible cartoon sweat beads from my forehead. Round one, down. Calm down, old chap, you'll be fine. "And how are you doing, my dear?"

"I'm doing just fine. What are you listening to?"

I glanced back at my stereo. "Um, right now I'm listening to Emperor."

"Emperor?"

"Emperor."

"Tell me about this Emperor."

That took me off guard. "Sorry?"

"I want to know about Emperor. I've never heard of them."

My mouth hung open. "You actually want me to talk. About heavy metal."

"Yup!" she chirped.

"Um . . . very well," I said. "But you asked for it."

"Oh, boy!"

I took a deep breath, closed my eyes, and began. "Emperor is a Norwegian black metal band, probably one of the most famous, if not *the* most widely acclaimed. They formed during the Norwegian black metal boom, a period in the late eighties and early nineties in Norway when a new brand of satanic, melodic, emotional, dark metal was springing up from the followers and listeners of old-school metal bands such as Venom, Celtic Frost, and Bathory. Emperor was part of the main roster of bands in Norway at the time, along with Mayhem, Burzum, and Darkthrone. They were implicated in some of the highly publicized church burnings and disappearances that occurred during this time period, and lost their drummer, Bård Eithun, when he killed a gay man one night in a park — which, by the way, is really fucking uncool, great band or not. Emperor's music became famous because of their knack for mixing the horribly brutal and the strangely beautiful. The album I'm listening to, *Anthems to the Welkin at Dusk*, is considered by most to be their pinnacle work, while I think the album following it, *Equilibrium IX*, is much better."

There was a *silence*. Not a pause, a *silence*. I could hear a cricket somewhere, and even the dusty rolling sound of a tumbleweed. Whatever she said next would show whether I was, in her eyes, *knowledgeable in my field* or a *total fucking dork*. That is, of course, if she was going to speak at all. *Any day now, Melissa . . .*

Uh-oh. A dork. I'm a —

"Damn, boy!"

My ears perked up like those of a dog who's just been told his food's ready, or a guy with a mullet who hears the first chords to Iron Maiden's "Run to the Hills."

"That was amazing!" she said. "You just gave me a *Rolling Stone* profile in thirty seconds! Where were you reading that from?"

I laughed nervously. "Wasn't. Just off of the top of my head."

"That is so *cool*," she said. "That you're so passionate about something, especially music, and you know that much about it! God! Can you do that for every band you listen to?"

"Uh, most of them."

"I am so impressed."

"Really?"

"Really." A pause this time. "Sammy Markus, you are to make me a mix."

"I am?"

"You are. I've never felt in better rock-and-roll hands than yours. I mean, if you can do this on the spot for one band, imagine what you could do with some time and a blank CD! Don't make it *all* growly-angry-hard music, but I definitely expect *some*, okay?"

I grinned. *MIX. MIXMIXMIX.* "Certainly, madame."

"Good." I could feel her smiling through the phone. "Now, if I heard you correctly, you were trying to arrange a second date with me when you called."

"Oh, yeah," I said. "So Saturday night I've promised my friends I'd hang out with them, but maybe I could see you during the day?"

"Splendid," she said. "I'm thinking we could maybe lie around on my bed for the whole afternoon listening to music, talking about life, and occasionally making out?"

What I wanted to say: "Sounds delicious, shweetums."

What I did say: "Ayuh."

"Good," she whispered. "Anyway, I should be getting back to my homework. But I'll see you then?"

"Yup. Yupyupyup."

She cackled. "Bye, Sammy."

"Yup."

The phone clicked in my ear. I carefully placed it in its cradle and strolled over to the center of my room.

And do you know what I did there?

Do you?

Well?

YOU'RE DAMN RIGHT I DANCED!

chapter 4
Procreation of the Wicked

I flipped open my CaseLogic and started fingering my way through the plastic pocketed pages. Everything I needed was at my fingertips.

Okay. Time to go.

Making a mix was something I loved, an activity I enjoyed more than most others. There's something about putting together a collection of music for someone that made me completely at ease with the world. Focusing all your thoughts and feelings about a single human being into a group of songs is a strangely cathartic experience. And of course there's that feeling you get later, when that special someone walks up to you and tells you they like some of the music that *you* chose for them. Just a blast. The definition of a natural high.

There are certain rules that apply to mixes, of course. Always start them off well — the first couple of songs are incredibly important. I personally preferred starting with a catchy, fun, sometimes softer track, something to draw the listener in. I put a harder, more energetic song as the second track, to really get out some of the meat of the mix. Always go out with a bang, too: Maybe not a hard song, but a powerful one should always close your mix. There are a few other rules usually only applying to anal-retentive mix-makers such as myself (I cannot make a mix with a sketchy or semi-decent track for track six or nine — don't ask me why, they just seem like important track numbers). How did I know all this? Simple: I had a lot of time, a lot of friends, and a lot of music. Therefore, I made a *lot* of mixes.

Now it was time for Melissa's Mix.

I started off with some soft rock (1. Tori Amos, "Siren") and followed it up with a little catchy hardcore (2. Blood for Blood, "Ace of Spades"). Now more metal: I skipped over all of my death metal (too growly and whatnot for a newbie), but grabbed a couple of thrash discs for here and there (3. Soilwork, "As We Speak"). Next, something nice and poppy, something to chill the listener out after listening to so much anger (4. Weezer, "No One Else"), but then another splash of hard rock to bring back the general feel of the mix (5. System of a Down, "Chop Suey!"). I grabbed some black metal to throw in — a little unholy Satan rock with a lot of keyboards was always a plus when it came to music for the ladies (6. Cradle of Filth, "Her Ghost in the Fog"). Back to the punk, making sure not to scare off the target audience with the harder stuff (7. Green Day, "One for the Razorbacks"), and some love-themed industrial (8. Stabbing Westward, "What Do I Have To Do?").

Track nine. Crap. What to put in for track nine . . . *who* to put in for track nine . . . gotta make it romantic, gotta make it alluring, gotta . . .

I got it. A little emo never hurts when it comes to romance, even if you feel like a tool for listening to it. Slapped it in and moved on (9. Saves the Day, "Hold").

Back to the anger, but with a nice beat behind it (10. Prong, "Snap Your Fingers, Snap Your Neck"), topped that off with some folky Goth (11. Marilyn Manson, "Lamb of God"). After that, some more black metal (12. Borknagar, "The Genuine Pulse") and a little more thrash (13. Testament, "Nightmare (Coming Back to You)".

Flipside that with an energetic punk cover (14. Pennywise, "Stand by Me") and follow it up with some female metal empowerment à la Nancy Sinatra (15. Megadeth, "These Boots"). After that, I hit it with a little lite punk with a personal message, just for my own sake (16. The Mr. T Experience, "Thank You (For Not Being One of Them)".

The next track was Slayer. I always tried to find someplace for Slayer on my mixes, simply because Slayer was my favorite metal band, and perhaps the greatest metal band in the world. They had the most energetic, angry, deep-seated, gut-searing, heart-grasping, head-banging songs in the world, and they made every one of them as catchy as the flu. Simply put, I spent most of my adolescence listening to Slayer, and I felt that it helped make me into the person I was. Without Tom Araya, Kerry King, Jeff Hanneman, Dave Lombardo, and Paul Bostaph, every bit of anger, angst, and rage in me would never have gotten out. Slayer saved my life. Period. Therefore, I threw some darker, more melodic Slayer in for the second-to-last track, something that was genuinely Slayer, but was still enjoyable to a metal newbie (17. Slayer, "Mandatory Suicide").

Now, to finish the sucker off. I needed a love song, but a rock song; a sad song, but a song that inspired a certain atmosphere of romance; a song to start out a relationship to.

I promptly hailed myself for being The Man. (18. The Smashing Pumpkins, "Stand Inside Your Love").

I pushed the CDs into my laptop, one after the other, letting them scan and finally burn. As this went on, I printed out a track list and cut it out for the casing, using the crappy lining that came with the blank disc as my guide. Mixes had been my Arts & Crafts projects for the last couple of years. There was nothing fleeting or half-assed in a mix when I made it — everything had to be perfect.

Next came the cover, which was possibly the best part of making the whole mix. I had always themed my various mixes with continuing ideas: the alphabet, shapes, animals, and so on. Right now, I was on Tarot. I had gone through a great deal of them already, drawing the stiff-figured, archaic Tarot drawings in my own cartoonish, dark fashion. So what to make Melissa? What Tarot card did she deserve?

I thought about her. About how she made me feel. About how much time I'd spent in the last two days just sitting at my desk and daydreaming about the feeling of her eyelashes when they brushed my cheek. A blinding flash of dreamy boredom flew back to me.

I did a bleak sketch of The World and slid it into the plastic. On top of the CD, I wrote *Alpha . . . Omega . . .* with a Sharpie marker, then popped the disc into its black casing.

There. Done. CD burned and labeled, cover drawn, track list written.

I glanced at the clock. 10:36 P.M. She lived on the Upper East Side, 86th Street, a cab ride away. I had school tomorrow. I could easily just call her and give it to her some other time. It'd be no big deal. Go to bed. Get some sleep.

I had my overcoat on in two minutes, and was out the door in seven.

chapter 5
Night Prowler

▷

Tuesday night, and I was amazed that I was actually doing this. Apparently, so was she. Her door opened, and she had this urgent look on her face like she'd expected me to remember which wire to cut, because otherwise the bomb would blow and the scarred villain would get away.

"I cannot *believe* you're here. Come in! Now!" Her hand yanked me in by my collar, and she slammed the door behind me.

"Missed you, too, darling."

"Hey!" she said, pointing at me. "I missed you fine without you calling me from a pay phone and showing up at my house for no reason. You *cannot* be here for too long!"

"Why not?"

"Because there's work, and, and I have school tomorrow, so you can't . . ."

She stopped talking because by then, I was up right in front of her, staring straight down into her eyes. She pressed herself against me and started breathing heavy.

". . . you can't . . ."

My arms folded around her waist, and my face got so close to hers that I could feel her breath on my lips and life was a fairy tale with me cast as the world's most unorthodox Prince Charming.

". . . oh . . ."

Soft but passionate, sexy but romantic. The best kiss I'd ever had. She placed her cool, soft hands on either side of my face and pulled me to her, the palms running slowly down my cheeks. And for that brief, warm, soft moment, everything else managed to melt away.

"Melissa, honey?" a voice called from down the hall.

The kiss ended suddenly, shattered. She looked in fear towards her parents' room and said, "Yes, Daddy?"

"Have you seen my keys?"

"Um, I'm not suuuure *gogogo*, did you check your jacket pocket *getinmyroom rightnow*?"

I bolted into her room, closing the door quietly behind me. Then I took a look around. A person's room says a lot about the person, just like his or her music. Pictures of Ewan McGregor, a Weezer poster (my mix was saved!), and various stuffed animals greeted me, as well as the wonderful underwear on the floor. A Post-it on the wall over her bed read *Melissa — Don't forget your math book!!! — Melissa* and one next to it flattered me; it had my name and number on it, with a word — *EEEEEEEEE!* — scribbled below.

I heard the door shut behind me and her voice whisper, "YOU should not BE HERE."

"I thought you'd be impressed with my romantic skills!" I said, turning to face her.

Christ, she was adorable when she was angry. She was standing there with her hands on her hips, jutting out into perfect points at the elbows. Her hair was all mussed, and she had this look on her face that screamed *I can't believe you* and *Come here right now* at the same time. Her smile curled up at one corner. That smile, I decided right then and there, was to be my eventual demise.

"This *isn't* a Shakespeare play, buddy," she chided. "I have a lot of work to do. You need to leave."

"I'll help you with your work!"

"I take chemistry," she purred, turning away from me, "not anatomy."

Yeah, I know. I nearly died of lust right there. I yanked open my bag and dug through it, finally managing to get out three words. "Mix. I have."

She stopped to stare at me like I was an alien, which was understandable considering I sounded like Yoda. I pulled a CD out of my bag and handed it to her. "Your mix. I made it. Here you go."

"Ooooh!" She scampered over, snatching it out of my hands and scanning the artists on it. I watched her eyes change their shape and direction, sometimes looking shocked, sometimes excited, sometimes just plain weirded out.

"Cradle of Filth? Prong?" She looked up, bemused and a little frightened at the same time. "*Borknagar?!*"

"The name's silly, but the song's really good. Trust me."

"I'm intrigued," she whispered, walking slowly towards me, her hands behind her back. "Showing up at my place so late to give me a CD . . . distracting me from my work . . . you are a bad influence, Samuel Markus."

"I try."

She was close to me now, her face a couple of inches in front of mine.

"Do you, now?"

A hand snaked up around my neck, caressing the side of my face. She bit half of her lower lip, and parts of my brain detached and attempted to slither out of my ears.

"So, do you, um, still want me to leave, 'cause —"

"Ssssh." She put her finger to my lips. "Silly boy. Come here."

I pulled her close in my arms for another moment of worldly bliss. We held each other tightly and tumbled onto her bed, giggling and touching and falling, caught in midair. Floating. I was floating, momentarily, with the girl I adored. Suddenly, God wasn't being his usual bastard deity self, and things weren't too bad, y'know. And now we were surrounded by mountains of fluffy, downy pillow.

Her head against my chest, her hand on my leg tapping out my heartbeat. I memorized it, took a photograph of the moment in my mind, and stored it away. She stroked my chest with her other hand and giggled.

"You're shaking a little," she whispered.

"I'm nervous," I mumbled. "My hands feel huge and my head's a blur —"

"There's a spike poking me in the back, deary."

"Exactly. Right there. Perfect example. This is so great, so wonderful, and I jab you with a steel spike."

"I like your spikes."

"I like spikes, too."

I suddenly wanted a fridge door to repeatedly slam my head in. *I like spikes, too?!* Why, because they're *pretty* like *flowers*, you ignorant simp?!

She didn't notice, choosing instead to stop beating out my pulse, and putting both of her hands flat against my chest. She sighed — not a world-weary, tired sigh, but a contented, things-are-good sigh. I was happy.

So I decided to say that. "I'm happy."

"You don't smile enough," was her response.

"What are you talking about?"

"I'm talking about you. You don't smile enough. You have a nice smile. So smile. Go ahead."

I smiled, and instinctively put my hand over my mouth. Ah-hah. My weakness revealed.

"And you see! You cover it up every time! It's not *fair!*"

"You're great."

"Mrrm. Thank you, dear. But you should still smile more."

"Run away with me."

"No. That's dumb. Be quiet."

I glanced down at her, disheartened. "That's a nice way to butcher some romance."

"Well, I mean, c'mon, hon. I couldn't just up and leave my life. I've got too many things here that I care about. I couldn't just run away from all of that. It'd be stupid."

Silence. Her logic nailed me. I was never one for the power of logic, instead allowing the power of goofiness, humor, and alcohol to take over. So I just lay there, staring at her ceiling and at how white it was, wondering what she was thinking. And as if on cue, she decided to tell me.

"Sammy?"

"Muh-huh?"

"Can I . . . I mean, there's kind of something I wanted to ask you."

More silence. She continued.

"I've always wanted a . . . a companion, basically. Someone who I could be with, who would take care of me, and talk to me, and be with me, like . . ."

"Physically."

"Right. Exactly. And I would, I would be that person's charge, basically. I would give myself to them, and they could look after me, and we could be together, and . . . yes. That's it."

"So, what you're saying is that we could be a . . . some-thing?"

"I would love to be a something with you, Sammy. I thought about it, and . . . can we? Please?"

I became part of a something. And as we lay there, with her hands and face on my chest, part of me did a little dance inside of my chest.

For once, being accepted didn't seem like such a bad thing.

chapter 6
Living After Midnight

Frank Sinatra's *Songs for Swingin' Lovers* is one of the greatest albums of all time, dammit. There's no arguing it. Anyone who claims otherwise has never listened to it, and if he or she has listened to it and doesn't like it, he or she is simply a moron. I mean, c'mon. Come *on*. There's more energy on that album than on any record made in the past twenty years (well, with the possible exceptions of Metallica's *Master of Puppets* or Slayer's *South of Heaven*). Every song makes you want to get up and dance. There's, like, the first song, "You Make Me Feel So Young," which is a happy-go-lucky whirl of childhood nostalgia, and then there's "It Happened in Monterey," which bleeds bittersweet unrequited love. The bass solos in "Too Marvelous for Words" are worth the whole damn $16.99 plus tax. And right when the record's about to get bad, in comes "Old Devil Moon" and "Pennies from Heaven." DAMN if it isn't one of the best records out there.

These were my exact thoughts as I strolled down East 86th Street between Lexington and Third. Frank was blasting into my ears, and life was good. My father always played *Songs* . . . to me when I was a kid, and it had stuck with me since. I used to think my dad was the coolest guy in the world, dancing around my living room to *Pet Sounds* and *Exile on Main Street*. (Come to think of it, I still thought that.)

"How About You?" dwindled down on my headphones, followed by the extended *EEEEP!* of my Discman, signaling the disc's final note.

Frank was great. A fucking god. May he rest in peace.

Now, the chaser.

Possessed, *Seven Churches*.

Chicken soup for the death-metal soul.

A badly played version of "Tubular Bells" spouted into my ear, followed by the grating, brutal, angry fathers of Death Metal. Furious drumming and shredding guitar work blistered my brain. Like washing down Smirnoff Ice with Jägermeister. Death (the band, mind you) needed to get off their high horse when it came to metal — these guys may not've been the first Death Metal band, but they may very well've been the best.

The city wrapped around me. New York is like that: It just engulfs everything inside of it, becoming whatever you want it to be. With Sinatra on, the city seemed older, classier. Now with Possessed destroying my brain cells, it was a dark, angry place, ready to be pillaged. And who better to do so than Conan?

35

I saw Brent standing with my little crew on the corner of Lex. With him were Irish, Pudgy (Liam, who we called Pudgy for the utter lack of fat on his body), Tygirl (Tyler, who we called Tygirl for his penchant for feelings and cream-colored sweaters), Mark, and Jamie. Brent, of course, was on his cell phone. Mark and Jamie, of course, were making out. Grinning, I cabbage-patched my way over to them. *Seven Churches* got me going strong. Tonight was gonna be good. I could feel it.

Irish saw me across the street and waved me over, telling the guys and Jamie that I was here. Pudgy and Tygirl waved. Brent acknowledged my existence by widening his eyes and ending his phone conversation. "Fucker!" he yelled as I sauntered through heavy traffic. "Where the hell have you *been* all day?"

"I was busy, that's all."

"Yeah, busy all right. Spent the day with the new girl, didn't ya, Sammy?"

I grinned. He was dead-on. I'd spent the *entire* day with Melissa. My fucking dream girl. I'd shown up at her place around ten-thirty in the morning and hadn't left 'til about six. We'd just stretched out there on her bed, talking and making out and yanking off each other's clothes and talking more. About everything. We taught each other: She explained *The Tempest* to me while I introduced her to Black Sabbath and Children of Bodom. She described the intricacies of Jack Kerouac while I told her about the murders and church burnings and the war between Mayhem and Burzum during the Norwegian Black Metal period of the early nineties. It'd been like that all fucking day: sharing our interests and ideas and passions and bodies. She was fun like the Murderdolls, but up close and personal like Strapping Young Lad, carefree like the opening of an Ozzy album, but layered and deep like an Opeth song. I liked this girl. A whole lot.

Brent caught my uncovered grin and smiled. "Aw, yeah!" he bellowed. "Sammy got the head!" That was Brent. A great friend and a fun guy, but a total misogynist and asshole about anyone he didn't know.

"Naw, it's not like that," I intervened.

"Jesus, you've only been talking about her all fucking week." Irish sighed cynically. "'Oooh, her hair, her skin, her body, nyah nyah nyah.' You little bitch."

"You're just jealous 'cause I'm getting some and you're not."

I felt hatred radiate from Irish as he gave me the Evil Eye. He hadn't gotten any for the past five months, and it was getting to him. That was our teasing routine: Irish got straight A's, so I was constantly reminded of the fact that I wasn't going to Yale. I, on the other hand, had an ability to get action when I really wanted to, so he was always reminded that he was the only person going near his own peepee. Grinning, I turned to them all and barked, "So! Ladies and gentlemen! What're we doing tonight?"

"Going to the park and getting fucked-up beyond belief," Pudgy replied, scratching the back of his head.

"Perfect," I said. "By the way, Jamie, I heard about Irish Saturday night — how're your shoes doing?"

Jamie shot me her winning smile, filled with venom. "Fuck you, Conan."

"Thought so."

I coughed violently, handing the devilish little thing back to Brent while at the same time trying to wave smoke out of his bedroom window. He took a massive hit and turned back to me. "'S good shit, right?" he managed to cough out.

I shrugged. I didn't feel any different. Tasted fine, I guess. I took it back and pulled another drag, feeling my throat burn up for a second time. Brent's instructions ran through my head: *Fill your mouth with smoke and then take a breath in. The smoke will sort of ride that breath into your lungs. Then exhale.* I blew out a massive puff of fragrant smoke, one that even Brent and Irish were surprised by.

"Dude," Irish said, taking it from me in pinched fingers, "is this really your first time?"

I nodded slowly. Why was that so amazing?

"Did you just never want to?"

I shrugged. "The opportunity never arose before, is all."

Irish took a deep drag and choked out, "Well, glad we're . . . enablers."

Brent laughed. "Enablers."

Heh. Heh heh. Enablers. That was pretty . . . pretty funny, actually . . . enablers . . .

"En . . . ema?" I said slowly, not quite sure why my face felt so heavy all of a sudden.

Brent and Irish stared at me for a second and then began to giggle uncontrollably. "Jesus, Sam, where the fuck did that come from?" bellowed the redheaded punk in front of me.

"Enema . . . 's a funny word . . ." tittered Brent.

"Dude," laughed Irish, "Ingmar Bergman!"

I began to laugh mindlessly, putting my hands over my mouth. My whole body was racked with the giggles. Ingmar Bergman? What was that? Why was it so fucking funny?!

"Bergman!" I screamed. "Bergman hamburger!" We fell to the floor laughing, Brent smacking his head on his bedside table on the way down. We lay convulsing on the carpet for another fifteen minutes, occasionally thinking of funny words like "vas deferens" and "monocle" to keep the laughter going. Finally, after the last giggle, Irish reached into his backpack and pulled out a forty-ounce bottle of malt liquor.

"Okay, boys, who wants a drink?"

I nearly tackled the fucker.

We sauntered our way to Fifth Avenue, discussing all things important: music, each other's mothers, what we intended to do to each other's mothers, how much school sucked, etc. Mark and Jamie walked towards the back of our group, their eyes connected in an iron grip, and suddenly I felt like patting Mark on the back and grinning at him and telling him how lucky he was, because I was feeling that way, too. I felt sorry for all the times I'd called him whipped, because it was just that he was happy with a girl. It was the same with the way we reminded Tygirl and Pudgy what bitches they were, but it was only because they had actual human emotions. They weren't cruel-ass preps like

Brent or cynical punks like Irish or crazy metalheads like me. They were just cool guys with feelings and we gave 'em shit for it.

⬜⬜

The girlfriend thing was always looked upon with furrowed brows among my friends and me. It was like, if you have one, bring 'er around so we can meet 'er, and then that's it. We don't want to see her again. Our friendly gatherings were always specifically separate from our romantic lives, and while none of us actually *said* that, it was just sort of common knowledge; nobody needed to say anything. (Even Jamie knew that — she had nearly lost one boyfriend who claimed she was ashamed of him when she refused to bring him around with us.) Some of us had tried, and it had always failed — either we hated the girlfriend or the girlfriend wasn't into our particular brand of humor. Irish once had a girlfriend who insisted on coming out with us one night, and was so disgusted by our "coarseness" that she left early. He broke up with her shortly after. There were exceptions, of course — Jamie had been our mutual friend for so long that when she and Mark started going out, she wasn't considered "girlfriend," she was just one of the guys. There was a saying we went by: *Bros before hos.* Girls were great, but your friends were what counted.

We made it to the park in no time, heading to a relatively isolated area somewhat downtown, which we called The Rock Park. It had these stone plateaus with bridges and ramps connecting them. Perfect place to get drunk or high. The first time we came here, I got so stoned that I started stumbling around, waving my fists and growling at anyone who came near me, occasionally barking, "I am barbarian!" That night, due to my spiked leather and intoxicated belligerence, I was given my nickname: Conan the Barbarian.

We climbed up onto one plateau of concrete and passed out the booze, which consisted of Georgi Vodka, Old English 800, Jack Daniels, and Colt .45. The bottle of whiskey made its way in a circle around us until it was drained, and then the beers were snapped from their plastic webbing. Brent passed out cigarettes, and all of us except for Mark had a smoke. Mark was cool like that. He didn't avoid smoking because it was bad for him, or because his parents smoked and he didn't want to be like them. He just chose not to do it. He was just a big blond kid who wanted only to play basketball and be with his girlfriend. And that was cool.

As the group dispersed, running around drunkenly and beating one another up, I sat down facing Mark and Jamie on the plateau. I grinned and slurred out, "Hey, gang!"

"Heeeey, Sam!" came the slurred reply.

"And how're you two kids doing?"

"Just fine, my friend, just fine," said Mark, who *never* got drunk, no matter how much he drank.

Jamie giggled tipsily. "I hear you've got a new girl, dude . . ."

"Yeah, she's great . . . I adore her. I *adore* her so fuckin' much. 'S great."

"Good for you, man. Good for you. She's all into your big Conanness?"

"Yeah . . . thinks the spikes're cute. 'S nice."

"Why, Sammy Markus . . ." giggled Jamie, "are you falling for a *girl*?"

"Y'know, I very well may b —"

Heavy hands grabbed the back of my overcoat and spun me around. Irish grinned excitedly into my perplexed face and screamed through his drunk exclamation of, "Dude!"

"Uh, I, uh, what?"

"Brent just rolled, like, the *fattest joint ever!*"

I howled, and me and Irish tumbled our way down from the concrete area where we stood, Mark and Jamie close behind us. We rushed out to where Brent stood grinning, holding a fat-ass blunt ready to be smoked. Pudgy was bouncing up and down singing something that sounded like, "Oh boy oh boy oh boy!" Tygirl couldn't stop laughing.

"Light that shit up!" shrieked Irish, nearly wrenching his Less Than Jake shirt off in anticipation.

Brent didn't have to be told twice. Our lighters flew one by one from our pockets, and we decimated that thing, three-tokes-and-pass style. Good shit, too — we were all coughing up a storm. The minute I exhaled my third drag, I felt my brain cells begin to pop. Pop. Pop pop pop. Pop goes the weasel. And the weasel goes fucking crazy.

Everything slowly turned into a rubber cartoon, and everyone seemed shorter. My legs had shrunk. How the hell could the sky and the ground close in on me like that?

The fattie was gone in about fifteen minutes, and we were gone with it. I stumbled over to Brent, throwing my arm around him, and mumbled, "Well, then . . . Bobby Urine Pants."

"Dude," Brent said, "I'm so fucking stoned."

"So am I, mein cheese!" yelled Pudgy, who was fighting Tygirl à la Godzilla versus Rodan.

"Then join the line!" I giggled, motioning with my one arm. Pudgy rambled over, throwing his arm around my shoulder. Tygirl followed, and then Irish. We had a regular drunk-line going, what with the five of us stumbling around and making mindless jokes. At one point, Irish fell over, screaming something about fetuses, but we picked him up and carted his ass along. Eventually, Jamie and Mark decided to go, hugging us good-bye and walking, with arms linked, to Jamie's place, our obscene hoots following them.

We walked, arms around one another's shoulders, uptown to our houses. Somehow we got started in a chorus of "How Dry I Am," which led to a round of "Back Your Ass Up," which led to the Dead Kennedys. By the end, we were just five drunk teenagers screaming, "Kill kill kill kill kill the poor!" It was great. The nights I lived for. Very metal. Very fun.

Brent and Tygirl split off from us around 71st Street. They lived farther uptown on the East Side, so we let 'em go with a handshake and a drunken profession of friendship. Me, Irish, and Pudgy hauled towards the 72nd Street Park exit, mumbling idiotic comments to one another about how incredibly gone we were.

And then we turned a corner and saw her.

She was leaning against the 72nd Street exit, talking to some girl I'd never seen before. They were giggling together, and then turned their heads, saw us, and froze. I tried to focus myself, but instead all I noticed was how big her eyes looked. Like an anime character. An image of her dressed in a school-girl outfit grinning and flashing the peace sign exploded in my head.

"Oh, shit! Hi!" I bellowed.

"Hey, fancy seeing you here!" Melissa looked at Irish and Pudgy hanging from my arms. "Who are these guys?"

I made quick, sloppy introductions. Pudgy made some sort of inebriated comment, but Irish just stayed quiet. He didn't look so good, all of a sudden.

Melissa introduced me to her friend, Kat, who reluctantly gave me The Pound. I grinned like an idiot, and finally managed to get out, "So, um, what're ya doing tonight, my magical girl girl?"

She looked at me funny. "Um . . . I'm just hanging with Kat. Hey, is your friend okay?"

"Who? Irish? Yeah, he's fine!" I glanced back at Irish, whose freckles had taken on a slightly green tint. "Dude, you okay?"

"Okay enough . . . to fuck some . . . bitches . . ."

"What?!" I wagged my palm at Melissa to tell her to wait. "Sorry, hold on one second." She tightened her face and nodded, visibly uncomfortable. "Irish, seriously, how're you feeling?"

"That kid's gonna pop," whispered Kat, looking at Irish as if he had demons coming out of his ears. "Like, any second now."

Melissa looked worried. "Well, I mean, I don't want to disturb you guys . . . I should —"

"Wait up, wait up, just a minute. IRISH! ARE! YOU! OKAY?!"

With great effort, Irish raised his head to look at me. "You heard me . . . I'm fine, you goddamn pig . . . screwin' . . ."

Melissa looked at Kat and mouthed the words "Oh God." I began to panic. "Sorry about this, he's just had a little much, is all. It's nothing, really. He'll be fine."

"Sam, it's fine, it's no big deal, me and Kat have to —"

"Nononononono!" I said. "No! He'll be fine. He's okay. It's cool." I was about to mention that this wasn't an uncommon situation for us, but decided that wouldn't help matters much. "He actually wanted to meet you, seeing as . . ." (Putting together a coherent sentence became rocket science and brain surgery at the same time.) ". . . he's heard so much . . . I mean, like, I've talked about us so —"

Irish jabbed a finger accusingly at Melissa. "Why're you freaking out so much, lady?" he spat, stumbling a few steps forward. "Sam, what's your little woman so . . . fucking scared of . . . afraid I'm gonna . . . throw . . . awr —"

As if on cue, Irish reeled to his side and puked everywhere. He didn't spit up or have dry heaves, he full-force **hurled**. A cheeseburger, five beers, and a quarter bottle of Jack went spilling all over the sidewalk, narrowly missing my dream girl's white sneakers. I giggled, blushing in embarrassment, and helped him out, patting him on the back and calling him a sick fuck.

Just then, I heard Melissa mumbling, "Right, I have to go. Bye, Sam," followed by footsteps. I pulled myself to my feet, wheeling around to try to follow her and leave Pudgy to help our sickly friend.

45

"Wait! Hey! Melissa!" I yelled after her. She never turned around. Not once. Just kept walking. I took a couple of steps towards her, but decided against going any farther once I registered how blurry and wobbly my vision was. Chasing her down would just put me in the same position as Irish. "Melissa! Please hold on!"

She turned around, frustrated. "How plastered are you?"

"What?"

"HOW PLASTERED ARE YOU?"

There was no right answer to that question. "A lot."

"Right. Go home, honey." She turned back around, shaking her head and striding away. I couldn't understand what had just happened. Finally, wasted and confused, I gathered up my friends and dropped them off at their buildings.

My walk home was miserable. I had no one to keep me company, and I was slowly coming down, which was never good. I tried to listen to music, but it didn't work — marijuana, alcohol, and Possessed didn't go well together. I stumbled my way up to my room, flung off my coat, and fell, fully clothed, onto my bed.

My head began rotating, and in it, I managed to get one line of thought going: *Where'd she go . . . she was upset . . . I fucked up, didn't I?*

The room spun out of control.

chapter 7
The Amen Corner

▷

Black Sabbath. I needed Black Sabbath.

My free hand flipped through my CD wallet. The other one was gripping my aching forehead, waiting for the Advil to kick in. *In the back. Your Sabbath CDs are in the back. Calm down.*

I yanked *We Sold Our Soul for Rock and Roll* out of its slot and pushed it into my stereo. The bells and rain sounded soft in the background, eventually giving way to Tony Iommi's pounding guitar. Blues-oriented stoned-out rawk with a dark undertone. Better for a hangover than a beer with Tylenol in it. I fell back on my bed, scrunching up my face in hopes that it would evaporate the razors running across my brain.

"What is this . . . that staaaands . . . before me . . ."

Jesus, Ozzy, heal my fucking brain. Sew it all up. How bad did I fuck up last night? I mean, I know I fucked up. But did she find it funny? Or endearing? Or is she as disgusted as I thought she'd be?

Back in ninth grade, at a New Year's party, I was with a bunch of friends from my old school. I mentioned that I intended to hook up with this girl later that night, and my friends all looked at one another and told me that I'd fuck it up. Trust them: I'd fuck it up. Why? *Because,* they said, *you fuck everything up. That's what Sam does.* In fact, for a while they called me Fuck-Up. And they all laughed, and I laughed, too, even though I felt this sinking black pit in my gut. I fuck up. That's what I do.

▷

". . . find out I'm the chosen ooone . . . oh NO . . ."

The phone split my head open. I stumbled from my bed and slumped onto my beanbag chair, yanking the phone to my ear and barking, "What?"

". . . hey."

I tensed. Melissa. Okay. Stay cool. Your head doesn't hurt that much. You'll be fine.

"Hey, honey, how are things?"

"I'm fine, everything's good. Kat just left."

"She stayed over?"

"Yeah."

"Oh. Cool."

We both shut up, wondering who was going to bring it up first. When I didn't respond, she went for it.

"So, about last night. Can we talk about that?"

"Yeah, geez, I'm sorry about that. Irish has a habit of puking when he has too much to drink. He's really a nice guy, honestly, it's just that he . . . I dunno, he drinks too much and throws up. Every time. I was kinda waiting for it."

Silence. Dead silence. The fuzzy hum of the phone hung blaringly in my ear. I had that sinking feeling in my chest, like I had just fucked things up royally, but I swallowed it. *Stay cool. You're doing fine.*

"Oh," she said softly.

Kill me.

"I mean, are you okay?" she asked. "You seemed pretty drunk last night."

"Yeah." I sighed. "Yeah, I'm okay. I've just got one of those really deadly hangovers, y'know?"

"Um, not really, actually."

"Sorry?" I was confused.

"I mean, I *don't* know."

I was beginning to get the gist of things, but before I could say anything, she asked, "So, have you had breakfast yet?"

We ended up at Manhattan Diner on 77th Street and Broadway. The Manhattan Diner was maybe my favorite morning-after breakfast stop: They had really filling, hearty meals that manage to soak up all the poisons in you, while the atmosphere of the place was nice enough that you could relax and enjoy yourself. Melissa had never been before, so I suggested we eat there.

I had waffles, bacon, cranberry juice, and coffee with massive amounts of sugar. She had some eggs and a bagel. We ate in silence for a little while, before I tried to piece together what she mentioned at the end of our phone conversation.

"You're straightedge?" I asked.

She looked perplexed and embarrassed. "I don't really know what that means . . ."

"Don't worry about it. It means that you don't drink or do drugs."

"Oh!" She looked relieved. "I didn't know there was a name for it. Yes, I am whatever-that-thing-you-said-was."

"Straightedge."

"Yes."

I sipped my cranberry juice. "Any specific reasons?"

"I got drunk at my uncle's wedding and started dancing crazily to 'Macho Man,'" she said, smiling. "Since then, anything that makes me dance to the Village People has been branded evil in my eyes."

I laughed. "Seriously, though."

Her smile fell, and she shrugged. "I don't know. They've always scared me a bit, I guess. I've seen some of my friends get drunk or high and do shit like dance on tables or puke into their own sneakers. Things they're ashamed of, y'know? The idea of losing control like that . . . it just doesn't appeal to me."

I nodded thoughtfully. I could understand that. For one thing, the sneakers thing hit a bit close to home. Thinking back on it, I'd made a right ass of myself last night — the desire *not* to do that seemed simple enough. "Does it make you uncomfortable that I'm not straightedge?"

She bit her lip. I took it as a yes.

I nodded again. "Because you don't like seeing *me* out of control."

She shook her head and I was lost. That wasn't the answer I'd expected. I leaned closer and asked, "Then what?"

"Well, I mean, it's partly that," she said, taking a bite of her bagel. "I will admit that I was kind of embarrassed for you guys last night. It was hard explaining to Kat how great you are after our little rendezvous." Her eyes shot up to me. "Is what's-his-name okay?"

"Irish? Yeah, vomit's, like, his best friend. Go on."

"But it's also . . ." And here she turned sort of pink and I wanted to die. "Whenever I hang out with my friends who drink or do drugs, they consider me sort of the *drag* sometimes, you know? Like, my sobriety, my wanting to stay clear right then, puts me in direct opposition to them. And I hate that."

"And you'd be unhappy if we —"

"— got like that. Exactly," she said. "Glad I could get that out. Geez."

It was strange to see someone who I knew as so set and strong in her opinion feeling uncomfortable trying to tell me something.

"I know it's early in a relationship to say all this," she said, "but I really *like* you, Sam, y'know? And it's weird for me not to fit in with a group, because I'm sort of used to fitting in. But if there's any person I don't want to be an outsider to, it's you." She looked at me pleadingly. "Does that make any sense?"

And by then, I couldn't stop smiling, because that was so

cute it almost cured my hangover (almost). I reached across the table and took one of her hands. "Y'know what? I'll try it for a while."

"Try what?"

"Going straightedge."

Now it was her turn to look surprised. "Well, Sam, I mean, you don't —"

"Sure I do. I mean, I agree with you on this one. The last thing I want to do is make you feel uncomfortable, or like an outsider. So, hey," I said, throwing up my arms, "if cutting the toxins out of my diet is a way to do that, I'll give it a try."

She looked incredibly happy. I knew I'd done the right thing.

"Thank you, Sam. That means a lot to me."

I shrugged and finished my coffee. "Anytime."

I paid the check and we got up to go. As we exited the diner, I stopped and stared hard at her. She looked defensively at me. "What? What is it?"

"Did you really get drunk and dance to 'Macho Man' at your uncle's wedding?"

Melissa went beet-red. "Sammy Markus, I swear to God, if you tell anyone about that —"

"'Macho Man,' of all songs!"

"I'll kill you! I'll stab you to death! I mean it!"

"Would you like me more if I dressed like an Indian? Or would you prefer a construction worker?"

"Smart-ass," she whispered, and grabbed my hand.

chapter 8
Enthrone Darkness Triumphant

More than a month passed, and Melissa and I only got closer. We ended up on the phone every night around eight-thirty (don't ask me why it was always eight-thirty; one of us always seemed to call the other around then for some reason) and we'd end up talking into the night. We would babble on mindlessly about things that really didn't matter, like ice-cream flavors and the radio stations we listened to as little kids. And when we weren't talking on the phone, we were walking in Central Park or reading aloud to each other or giving each other obscenely large hickeys. We were teenagers in puppy love. It was revoltingly sweet.

I started hanging out with my school friends less and less, but it didn't really bother me, and they never mentioned it bothering them. After a while, the only friends I really saw outside of school were Brent and Irish, and even then I wasn't spending half as much time with them as I used to. Sometimes I would register that they were showing up less frequently in my life, but I dismissed it. Melissa became their new ammunition in our endless war of moronic insults: They were sick of hearing about her, they didn't need to know this much about her, they'd show her what a real man could do, and so on. I figured that if they were having so much fun ragging on me about her, they were doing all right.

The more Melissa and I hung out, the more she wanted to know about metal. It fascinated her — mainly, I suppose, because she knew absolutely nothing about it. And by *nothing*, that's exactly what I mean: She finally swallowed her pride and admitted that the only Metallica song she could identify by name was their cover of Bob Seger's "Turn the Page." (I know, I wanted to dismember a ballerina after I heard that.) Slowly, I started introducing her to the culture, the different kinds of metal, and the great leaders of the genre. It took some work, but I managed to use what little she knew about rock and roll to twist it to my advantage, until one day I found myself saying, "Well, Lemmy is basically the Bruce Springsteen of metal . . ."

Time went by. It was working. I was content.

▷

"Oh my God. What is *that*?"

"This," I said, holding up the CD for her to see, "is Cannibal Corpse's *Butchered at Birth*. An excellent death metal album, if I say so myself."

She stared, wide-eyed, at the carnage-soaked cover, turning

away after a few seconds. "Jesus," she gasped, "that's *horrible*! My God, how could anyone *enjoy* something like that?"

I shrugged. "It's a good album. The song with Glen Benton on it is really fun."

"Glen Benton?"

"Y'know. The singer in Deicide."

"Oh, yeah," she said, rolling her eyes, "*that guy*. I completely forgot. Deicide. Right."

"Hey, you wanted to come shopping with me!"

We stood in the front section of Generation Records, a small record shop on Thompson down in Greenwich Village, about a block away from Washington Square Park. I came to Generation all the time, due to its small yet obscure heavy metal section. It was one of the two shops I went to whenever I was looking for that one death metal or black metal CD that I couldn't find anywhere else. Melissa had jumped at the chance when I called her and invited her to go shopping with me, not knowing that in this case *shopping* exclusively meant record shops and spiked-jewelry stores. She seemed interested in the places we were going, but in the same way people are interested at a zoo or a museum.

"Yeah, well . . . you don't need to be thrusting *disgusting* album art in my face!"

I leaned back from the rack and kissed her. Her tongue flickered into my mouth, and I pulled away, grinning. "You're wonderful," I whispered.

"So are you," she said sweetly. "So, what're you doing next weekend?"

"Um, Friday night I'm going to a concert, and then I'm free Saturd —"

"What concert?"

"Um, Deicide. The band I mentioned earlier."

"Oh, yeah? Cool. Can I come?"

The words hit me like a brick. "What? Come to the show?"

"Yeah!" she chimed in. "You always talk about how 'sick' or 'bitching' these concerts are. I want to see you there. Y'know, in your element."

The words caught in my throat. I wasn't quite sure whether this was a joke or not. I mean, this was, like, a dream. This girl, who was totally crazy about me, was interested in something I loved. She considered my little obsession with metal music as something other than a punch line. It was good. It was perfect. Speak up, dammit! Finally, the tracheal dam broke and I sputtered out, "Oh, yeah! I mean — sure! I'll pick you up at your place!" Looking back at the rack, I smiled and said, "In fact . . ."

I bought her a copy of Deicide's *Serpents of the Light*, my vote for their best album, to get her used to their music. She winced at the cover at first, but finally slid the CD into her pocket with a "thank you." We walked out the door with the ding of a bell, and headed through Washington Square Park.

◁◁

I slumped down on the porch of my bunk at camp and carefully clicked the disc into place in my CD player. The sun had begun to set in the distance, turning the sky into a mountainous landscape of fiery orange. I closed the lid and pressed the PLAY button, listening to the sharp beep of the Discman and the quick whirring of the CD inside.

I glanced at the cover again while waiting for the music to kick in. What the hell was this supposed to be a picture of, anyway? It looked like . . . well, I had no idea. Like a skull with no mouth and an inverted cross jammed into the top of it. Ridden by a bunch of demonic little imps. Sinking into a river of blood. Surrounded by a bunch of satanic churches. Churches with —

The first notes cut in and I stopped. I froze and listened.

This was . . . oh, wow. This was different. This. Wow.

It was . . . dulcet. Dulcet and demonic at the same time. Notes slowly drifted into my ears, strange, moaning notes that reminded me of weeping. Slowly, a drum roll kicked in, and the entire sonic force hit me.

"An unforeseen future nestled somewhere in time, unsuspecting victims — no warnings, no signs . . ."

This wasn't Nine Inch Nails or Nirvana or even Rob Zombie. Between the wrenching sounds of the guitars, the pounding gunfire-drums, and the diabolical vocals, something new, dark, and powerful poured into my ears. All of a sudden, I knew why some parents were scared of this music, why they believed it was a call to violence and devil worship. And I loved it.

"Judgment Day, the Second Coming, arrives . . ."

Wow. This was so evil. So wonderfully evil.

"Before you see the light . . . YOU MUST DIE!"

I sat back and watched the orange clouds, now imagining them to be alive with fire, like Heaven was being burned to the ground by its overpowering opposition from below. I felt liquid shadow drip out of my every pore, and right then I would've given anything to soar up, wings spread, pitchfork in hand, and watch the pearly gates immolate in all their hypocritical glory.

Slayer. Oh, wow.

"So," she asked as we walked through the park, gripping my arm and pulling close to me, "have you always been into the metal thing?"

"What do you mean?"

"Well, I mean, you seem so used to it, so confident. It's like you're wearing an old suit. You feel good in it. You *look* good in it."

"Nah, I wasn't always into the 'metal thing.'"

"What? Your brother get you into it?"

"Carver? God, no. He was always into punk and hardcore, but never a metal fan. He's the middle ground of the family — I love satanic death rock, Erica likes dime-a-dozen pop, and he likes music that's somewhere in between. The metal thing just sort of happened around seventh grade."

"Explain."

I thought for a second, then continued. "I was always really into horror movies, right? I still am. I'm a total horror buff. But not as much anymore. Horror was great to me because I loved monsters. I like watching vampires and demons and were-wolves and zombies and everything. They were cool and foreign and . . . dark. I loved the dark."

"Sounds like good old you."

I shrugged. "I've always liked the darker side of things. I've always been a bit angry at the world."

"Why?"

I paused, thinking about it, but then finally deciding to leave it for later. "Something happened to me."

"You wanna talk about it?"

"Later." I felt my head bow, felt it look down and away from her. "Please, not now."

"Okay."

"So, um, anyway . . . um . . ."

"Monster movies, darling."

"Right. Monster movies were all I really cared about until about seventh grade. On the way home, in the beginning of October, I stopped into a Sam Goody to get my mom a CD, and I saw *Hellbilly Deluxe* by Rob Zombie, and I thought, 'Wow . . . the musical equivalent of a horror movie!' I mean, I'd been listening to some harder rock, like Nine Inch Nails and newer Metallica and the Offspring, but this was totally different. Pentagrams, monsters, the whole shtick. I went home, I put it on, and I was just blown away. It amazed me. And from there, it only got darker." I threw on a malicious grin. "Slayer was the band that really did it for me, though. Slayer was like Rob Zombie, only without the camp value and with better musicianship. They scared the hell out of me at first, and I loved it. Pure fucking *evil*."

"Huh!" she said as we sat down on one of the benches in the middle of the park. In front of us, skaters whooshed around the large, Roman forum-esque structure in the park's middle, listening to some oi punk band and laughing mindlessly. One of them had a headful of graying dreadlocks; he looked like a mop being thrown this way and that.

"Yeah." I thought a bit. "I guess it all tied into my love for horror. I mean, with horror movies, you could create monsters, right? But with heavy metal . . . you could *be* a monster. You could get up onstage and *be* the Antichrist for a few hours, all

59

the while making some kickass music. When I first saw pictures of Kerry King or Dimebag Darrel, they looked to me like characters out of a comic book. And that appealed to me. I spent most of my childhood reading comics, wanting to be a super-hero or a powerful villain. And with heavy metal, it was like I could *be* one."

"Wow," she said, "that was genuinely beautiful! I'm stunned!"

"Why . . . thank you, dear!"

"Not many people could put together that deep a statement about someone named 'Zombie,' dear."

"Well, not many people could stop me from tickling them, either."

"What?!" she squealed as my hands dived for her waist.

chapter 9
More Human Than Human

▷

We went back uptown and settled into her house, munching Pirate's Booty and sipping cranberry juice. Her couch was one of those black leather-but-not-quite deals that was simply asking to be slacked on, with huge, puffy cushions facing a massive TV. All around us were tall windows looking out onto the Upper East Side.

"Is this okay?" she asked, popping a piece of Booty into her mouth, looking a little afraid.

I nodded. "Why wouldn't it be?"

"Well, y'know, if you want to, like, do something more out and about, we can . . . if you want to and all."

I made circles with my index finger on her thigh. "Don't worry about it, darlin'. I'm fine with juice and snacks in the living room."

"Okay," she said, looking a little reassured. "I don't know. I'd hate to be a boring companion."

"You're not. Trust me. You're not."

We went silent for a bit. She was biting her lip in that cute little way, where half of the lip sticks out from under her teeth and the other half is being bitten, like someone on the movie poster of a romantic comedy. And I wanted to talk about things, or kiss her, but I couldn't get my mind off of what we'd talked about earlier.

"I, uh," I stammered, "I don't tell a lot of people about my childhood."

Her eyebrows went up, the lip sliding out from under her canines to reveal simple gritted teeth. She nodded, putting a hand on my leg, and said, "Take your time, honey. I'm here."

"It really wasn't . . . fun, y'know? Wasn't stable, right?"

Another pause.

"I'm listening," she said softly, genuinely concerned.

"I mean, I got bullied a lot, right?" Dammit, there it was. The lump in the throat. Next, there'd be stinging eyes, and off I'd go into another cliché. Suck it up. "I got teased a lot, and everything, and some worse stuff, right?" I gulped, then continued. "Like, once a kid hit me in the back of the head with a brick."

"Jesus," she whispered, her hand touching my arm. I suddenly realized that I was sitting in a fetal position. Christ, not this again. *Suck it up*.

"Yeah, a brick. And I got beaten, like really beaten regularly. A lot of pain. This one kid, he tore up one of my drawings and, and, he made me eat pieces of it, right? Eat it real slow. It, heh, it tasted fuckin' *terrible* . . . but, y'know, that was grade school, right? Everyone got teased and everything . . ." I took a breath, and decided to go for it. "But you have to be strong, you know? Right? Being strong is all that mat —"

And I just broke. I couldn't tell her about any more of it, about the black, angry thing inside of me that squirmed and screamed and never went away. I wanted to tell her so badly, and instead I just started crying harder than I'd cried in a while. I just sobbed in that scrunched-up ball with snot and tears running down my face, and sweat breaking out on my forehead. (Did anyone else sweat while they cried? For me, it was like clockwork . . .). I wanted to stop, to wipe my face off and apologize and maybe make a joke or leave or something that would help, and I couldn't. I just could. Not. Stop. Crying.

And it's like she wasn't repulsed at all. She just draped herself over the little quivering ball of me, and her arms clutched me, and she put her head on my shoulder. I felt her hand going through my hair, and her voice cooing, over and over again, "Shhhh . . . it's okay, just cry . . . it's okay, just cry . . ." like a mantra. After a while, I managed to unlock one of my arms and grasp one of hers. My sobbing died down to me just softly crying, shaking, trying to recover my senses. I just wanted to stop, and I couldn't, and she didn't care. She just kept running her hands through my hair and telling me to cry. And about that time, I wondered why I hadn't found her before now. Jesus Christ.

Finally I stopped. We didn't say anything for a while; me because I was too embarrassed, her because she must have been waiting for me to say something. At last I managed to blurt out, "Fuck, I'm sorry."

"Oh, Sammy."

"I'm so sorry. Christ. Some guardian I am."

"You're a wonderful guardian. You just needed that, is all."

I mumbled, "I've never really, I dunno, I've never talked to anyone about it before. The bullying, the beating, all —"

"Sssh. It's okay. You don't have to."

"But I just thought I should tell you, I mean, I really care —"

She kissed me lightly on the temple. "Oh, hey, come on. You don't have to tell me *everything*, especially if it hurts you this much. Not all at once. I'm not going anywhere, silly." There was a little pause, and then she asked, "Who else have you told this to?"

And it hit me that I hadn't really told anyone about most of it. I'd gushed to Carver a couple of times about some of it, and I'd talked to my parents about it once in a while, but that was it. Irish and Brent didn't know, though I could tell they knew *something* crappy had happened to me as a kid. None of my other girlfriends really knew. I'd pretty much kept a lid on that side of myself.

But here I was with a girl I'd been dating for a month and a half, and I was telling her about things that scared me as soon as I thought of them. There was no apprehension about feeling weak in front of her, none of the worries that she'd find me whiny or stupid. I'd spent years afraid that everyone, especially girls, would just sneer and say, "Get over it, Sam." And yet here was my girlfriend of a few weeks letting me cry on her shoulder, taking on what I thought no one else would care about. It was a little scary, but . . . comforting. At long last, I'd found someone who I could trust and believe in that much. I finally managed to say, "My brother. And . . . one or two other people."

I gulped again, and we were silent.

"Sam, you're special," she said quietly, staring at the blank screen of the TV and running her knuckles down my face. "You're a special person. I didn't *know* what happened to you as a kid before today, and even then I could see that you're a special person. If not for anyone else, then for me, okay? So don't think this doesn't make you my guardian. I mean . . . I've only known you a few weeks, and you already matter so much to me. It's a little strange, I know, but in the end, I don't care. You're just so *fucking special. That's* why I wanted you to stop drinking and doing drugs. *That's* why I wanted you to take me downtown today, y'know? You're so special, and I want to see that. I want to see it and preserve it and watch it thrive."

I managed to get out a laugh. "I'm just your crazy heavy-metal boyfriend, Melissa."

And that was when it changed. All of a sudden, she moved around so that her face was right in front of mine. She stared me dead straight into the eyes and said, "No. You're not. Got that?"

I nodded, unsure of what she meant.

She elaborated: "You are *not* some fucking character, okay? You're someone. You're a special *person*. And if anyone tells you otherwise, I'll destroy them. You're *not* just another Goth, and you're *not* an idiot boy toy. You're Sammy Markus and you're special. So don't give me that shit."

I nodded again, smiling a little. "Thanks."

She smiled back. "Anytime."

We kissed really softly. And everything was right, you know? 'Cause she was the first person who didn't make me a china doll or a basket case or the elephant in the middle of the living room or whatever. She treated me like me. And that was pretty cool.

chapter 10
Total Disaster

Wednesday, English class with Dr. Bersner. Me and Brent were acing the class, anyway, so Brent got into what he does best: passing judgment.

"I don't like it. I think it's a bad idea, dude. Don't."

I stared dreamily into space, barely hearing him, trying to concentrate on Dr. Bersner as he talked about Baudelaire.

"Wanna know why?"

"Nope."

"I'll tell you why. She's a nice girl. Preppy girl. My kind of person." I glanced over and had to agree with him. Brent was the preppiest of my close friends, and while Melissa wasn't exactly the Fitch to his Abercrombie, she was preppier, much preppier, than I was.

"Yeah, well," I said, looking at him sideways, "she's your kind of person. And you're my friend. So I guess it works out."

"Yeah, I'm your friend. I'm your friend who *tolerates* having to listen to the Haunted when we hang out. I'm your friend who can hardly even make devil horns with my hands." Brent shook his head. "She's gonna hate the music, she's gonna hate the atmosphere, and she's gonna get angry or worried or something."

"Piss off. It'll be fine."

"Dude. She might get *hurt*. I remember when you took me to see that band Shadows Fall, and I got punched in the face in the middle of the mosh pit. My chin was sore for weeks. C'mon."

"She won't get hurt," I hissed, "because I'll be watching her the whole time. Besides, you're a whiner at heart. The guy didn't even hit you that hard."

"He punched me! In the *face!*"

"Anyway, she told me she wanted to try going into the pit."

"Really? No shit? Wow. She seemed mousier to me."

"Piss off, Brent."

"Big breasts, though. Really nice ones."

"Piss off, Brent."

"You think the fact that she wants to mosh is a sign that she gets violent while —"

"Okay, Brent, leave it alone!"

Dr. Bersner stopped talking and looked over at us. "Ahem, um, Mr. Markus, is there something more *entertaining* than 'Paris Spleen' at this moment?"

"No, Doc," I said.

"Uh-huh. I'm sure. So you won't mind *telling* me, um, what the poor boy's toy is."

"A rat."

"Good job, Mr. Markus." Doc smiled. "Good student. Weirdest kid I've, um, ever taught, but you know your Baudelaire." He gave me an approving little nod; then, turning to Brent, he said, "So, um, Mr. Bolmen, what exactly does Baudelaire wish to, um, *do* to the poor, in, um, 'Paris Spleen'?"

Brent looked dumbfounded. I whispered out of the side of my mouth, "Beat them up."

Brent smiled. "Beat the shit out of them, Doc."

"Good job, um, Mr. Bolmen. Watch your language."

⬜⬜

I hated how Brent did that. It was weird. He was one of my best friends, but in the end, the dichotomy was amazing. On the one side is a short, awkward, antisocial, overweight kid wearing spiked leather and an Iron Maiden T-shirt who, on the inside, is really just a big teddy bear. On the other side is this tall, handsome, scrawny, slick, preppy teenager in sunglasses, who is without a doubt one of the outright meanest sonsabitches on the planet. He just did what he wanted, regardless of who got hurt. Our only real noticeable bond was the occasional band (he liked Rob Zombie, while I didn't mind Prodigy now and then), a penchant for wearing black (him casually, I satanically), a love of marijuana and alcohol, and a hatred of authority. Somehow, it had worked out perfectly.

The day at Melissa's came back to me, and I began to stew it over: Why *hadn't* I told Brent and Irish and my other close friends about all the bad shit that used to happen to me? Why had it been so easy for me to release it all in front of Melissa, while the idea of doing the same thing in front of Brent and Irish set off a big, red VERBOTEN! sign in the back of my head? Maybe it was just some sort of built-in masculinity thing, where I'd feel like the wimp . . .

. . . or maybe it was because I didn't feel like it was necessary. I was pretty sure they'd understand — as I'd told Melissa, I thought they had their suspicions that my childhood was fucked up and painful. In the end, it felt like they didn't need to be told, that it would be redundant. It wouldn't change anything; they wouldn't treat me any differently or be upset by it. It was unspoken: They were my friends no matter what, and would be there for me no matter what. We didn't need to do anything to prove it.

Now, turning back to me, Brent said, "Here: You go to the Deicide show, and *I'll* take care of Melissa for the night."

"Don't worry about it, buddy-pal," I told him, "I'll be fine. 'Sides, aren't you planning to hook up with that Abbie girl Friday night?"

"Solid. Closure. She broke up with me, so I'll convince her I've changed, hook up with her, aaaaand dump her like a sack of trash."

"God, you're sick. Smart, but sick."

"Y'think she cheats on you?"

BAM! A sledgehammer covered in nails hit me in the chest. I turned to Brent, one eyebrow raised, and snapped, "No. 'Course not."

"No?"

"No way." Thinking about it for a second, I mumbled, "Hell, man, that was uncool."

Brent looked puzzled. "How so?"

"What am I supposed to say to a question like that, Brent? What am I supposed to do, other than get upset?"

"You're upset?"

It hit me that Brent had no idea why the question would upset me. I tried to explain. "It seems like you're making an affront towards our relationship, y'know? Like, questioning how we feel about each other."

Brent shrugged. "So?"

Now he was just being an idiot. "SO, that's not cool! Why would you question our loyalty like that?"

"Because I . . . don't know," he said slowly, obviously thinking it over. "Like, honestly, I don't really know how this thing happened between you two in the first place." He glanced over at me. "Like I said, Conan, she's my kind of person, y'know? Part of a preppy crowd. And I know I'm your friend but, man, me trying to be your *girl*friend would just be weird."

I managed a smile. "It certainly would."

"Bolmen! Markus!" yelled Doc. "Pay attention, dammit!"

"Sorry," we both said, and went back to talking.

"I just don't trust this concert thing, you know?" he continued. "It might be fun and educational and all that, but it also might just, you know, drive those differences between you home." He looked over at me, trying to salvage the conversation.

"I mean, the cheating comment, I was just wondering. Like, honestly. I figure, you two are so different — maybe she does. Maybe you're, like, her *bad boy*. I don't know. Forget it."

⬚⬚

I had taken Brent to the Shadows Fall show to get him drunk and rock him out, which we certainly ended up doing — Brent hadn't even felt that punch until the next day. But translating that over to a romantic context didn't work as well. It dawned on me that taking Melissa could, in fact, turn out to be a big fucking train wreck. But every time I considered calling it off, something roared in the back of my head: *You idiot! A girl, a girl who you* like, *has offered to come to a fucking* DEATH METAL SHOW *with you! She* wants *to go! Don't blow it!*

As for the cheating thing . . . I wasn't going to even consider that. I trusted her.

▷

I sighed. "Well, I'm sure the concert will be fine, and I don't think she cheats on me. I trust her. If she does, you'll be the first to know."

The minute I said it, I wanted to take it back. Brent smirked and said, "Yeah, I bet I will, son!"

"I hate you. I'm getting new friends."

"Me and Melissa gonna get all freaky and *nasty*!" He looked over at me with a grin, to which I responded with a glare that could burn granite. Brent softened. "Look, dude, just keep your eyes on her. That's all. Don't, y'know . . . get screwed over or anything."

"I won't. Thanks. Asshole."

Doc dismissed us. I walked out of class, away from Brent, trying to shake off a sense of worry and nervousness that weighed heavier on me than my backpack.

It didn't work. Lunch tasted sour.

chapter 11
Bring the Noise

▷▷

As Melissa and I walked up the subway steps on Friday night, I pulled a cigarette from my coat pocket and popped it between my lips. I offered her one, but she turned it down. "I've decided to quit," she said.

I shrugged, lighting mine and dragging deep.

"Sam?"

I looked over at her. She gave me a look, one of those *C'mon . . . you know . . .* looks, as if there was something I was forgetting, something that I was supposed to be doing. My eyes darted from side to side, and I finally said, "Um . . . yes, Melissa?"

"Well, I'm quitting smoking."

"Okay."

"Well?"

". . . Good luck, I'm glad. Healthy choice. No cancer for you."

She sighed. "Well, it's gonna be kind of hard for *me* to quit smoking if I taste a cigarette every time I kiss you."

I froze. There were two options running through my mind. One of them was slightly absurd, but the other was just plain bad. I went with the former:

"Yoooou want me to start carrying around gum at all times?"

She laughed. "No, Sam."

I took another drag and thought harder. "Tic Tacs?"

She laughed again, this time with less zeal.

"Those little Listerine strip thingies?"

She didn't laugh. Like, she reeeally didn't laugh. Her face was all seriousness. "Sam. Come on."

"You want me to quit smoking?!" No. No no no. What next? No Tylenol?

She nodded slowly, giving me a smile. I didn't like it, but at the same time, it was sort of . . . endearing. Her smile read, *Stupid little boy. This is why I date you.*

"But . . . but, Melissa! C'mon! Why?!"

"Because it's not good for you. And because I want to. I really want to. And I need your support with this. I need you to help me quit. And if you're smoking around me, it certainly won't help. Please? For me?"

"I . . . I . . . I mean, why can't you —"

And then I looked into her face and I remembered the past week. Shopping downtown, giggling at each other's jokes, holding each other in her room, tearing each other's clothes off in mine, on the phone every day after school, how wonderful she

74

was . . . and I knew I had to sacrifice it. My love of cigarettes didn't matter. Hell, my happiness didn't matter. Forget my happiness. Who was I? A metalhead idiot. She was wonderful. *Don't fuck up.*

". . . Yeah. Okay, I'll do it."

"Really?"

"Yeah. Yeah, for you. Geez, the things I do for love. . . ."

She grasped my face, pulled me to her, and kissed me deep. Just as I began to snake my arms around her waist, she pulled away and chimed, "C'mon, we're gonna be late."

I walked with her. We strolled away from New Utrecht station towards L'Amour, New York's rock capital.

⬚⬚

L'Amour is a tiny club in Bay Ridge that was famous for being around throughout the Great Eighties and showcasing some of the best and brightest of the heavy-metal scene, making it the CBGB's of heavy metal. All the greats had played there: Metallica, Death, Morbid Angel, Twisted Sister, Megadeth, King Diamond, Dark Angel, Celtic Frost, Sepultura, Testament, Possessed, the mighty Anthrax, and, of course, the all-powerful Slayer. It now showcased all of the biggest extreme metal bands who weren't big enough to fill the larger concert venues in Manhattan, like Irving Plaza or Roseland. I had seen an endless number of bands there, but never Deicide. Never. And I was a big Deicide fan.

Tonight was going to be special.

"Don't you love it?" I inhaled the autumn air deep into my lungs.

"What?"

"Bay Ridge. I love it. Always have. I've spent my entire life in the yuppie section of the Upper West Side, when really I've just wanted to hang out in places like this."

She smiled slightly. "Um . . . are you serious?"

"Yeah, why?"

"Well . . . I don't know." She motioned to a boarded-up window covered with graffiti. "It's just . . . kind of run-down and foreboding. A little seedy."

"Seedy?! Bah! How dare you?!" I scoffed, pulling off a pose straight out of *Hamlet*. "Bay Ridge of Brooklyn is the fairest of all realms in New York!"

"You really think that?" She arched her eyebrow.

"Nah," I said, standing back up. "It's basically a big monument to car washes and auto mechanics. But I love it."

The closer we got to L'Amour, the giddier I got. I hadn't been to a show in ages. I could already smell the club, the cigarette-armpit-sweat-booze-electricity smell that came with every concert. I grinned childishly, trying to listen to Melissa as she talked to me about shoes. She didn't understand. She would, though. Finally.

The minute she saw the crowd in line at the show, she tensed up. Her hands went from shakily playing with something on her jacket to being crammed into her pockets. Her shoulders were closer to her temples than normal. She didn't just seem nervous, she seemed frightened. These people, this situation, the whole thing was scaring her.

At first, I was flooded with . . . well, annoyance. Why was she scared of these people? They didn't care. They didn't judge. It didn't really matter what you wore or how you looked to them; it was about the music. They were people, like us. Just because they looked a little different and dressed a little strangely didn't make them scum and villainy. But the annoyance was washed away by gratitude: She was uncomfortable in the situation but was doing it for me, anyway. That was enough. She wanted to see my world, and for that, I could deal with a little fear.

We walked down the line of long-haired death-obsessed kids pouring out of the door. They smoked, snarled, and chortled loudly, all of them ready for the coming chaos. I always felt a little weird at these shows, though: Deep inside, I couldn't help feeling like the richie boy-brainiac character, y'know? Like, I grew up a privileged child with a good education, and that somehow made me a bigger pussy than the rest of these kids. One time, at a show, a girl I'd just met commented that I must've had really good braces, because my teeth were all straight. I nearly died of embarrassment. It was weird. Even among the exiled, I never really felt at ease.

Melissa looked up at me timidly and tittered. "Quite the motley crew here, huh?"

"Crüe sucks!" bellowed a huge Hispanic kid in a Darkthrone shirt, snarling happily at her. I cackled a bit, pushing him back and giving him The Pound. "Shout at my *asshole!*"

"But they wrote a song about you!" Melissa said in a mock-sympathetic voice.

The kid looked confused. "What, 'Looks That Kill'?"

Her smile turned mischievous. "No, 'Bastard.'"

We contined walking to the back of the line, trailed by a chorus of laughter and someone saying, "Oh, dissed!" Melissa looked up into my eyes and smiled nervously. "I did good, huh?" she asked.

I couldn't stop the warm feeling from welling up and filling my bones like a good shot of tequila. "Honey, you did great. *Damn*, that was hardcore."

"You've taught me well," she said, nuzzling into my shoulder. "Are all the kids at this show going to be like that?"

"Well, just be ready for that kind of stuff and a lot more. This place is all about Dionysian frenzy and reckless abandon."

She whirled her face to me, a quirky smile across it, and said, "All about *what*?!"

I chuckled. "Dear, just because we're metalheads doesn't mean we're stupid. We know what 'reckless abandon' and 'Dionysian frenzy' are, okay?"

"I wasn't . . . well . . . I know *you're* smart . . . but it's not the most *intellectual* music, you have to admit . . ."

"Is, too!"

"Is not! Any genre with that many songs about Satan . . ."

"And that many songs about Elizabeth Bathory . . ."

"Elizabeth who?"

"Exactly," I said, moving her forward and into the club.

chapter 12
The Toxic Waltz

▷

The smell hit me before I exited the blackened hallway. Nicotine, electricity, sweat, blood, booze, hair, cotton, leather. This was gonna be so great. SO great. I was taking her to a metal show, a Deicide show no less!

"Smells like an armpit," she said.

"It does not! It smells great! It smells like . . . like . . ."

"Like death?"

I grinned a big, idiot, hyena smile. "Like heavy metal."

She took a deep breath and smiled. "Poetry, honey. Truly."

We stood against the side of the bar platform at the edge of the pit, making small talk and throwing little quips back and forth. It was sort of cute how we could always do that — we had just enough ridicule to make the relationship interesting. She would ask me how my day of destruction and devil worship was, while I'd tell her how pretty she was, considering she was a mainstream whore dancing for The Man. God. Finally. A girl like this. She was different from me, yeah, but . . . but she was great.

I felt her hand latch onto my arm as a dude covered in studded leather from head to foot brushed against us.

I glanced over at her. "You a little scared?"

She shook her head, though it was obvious she felt out of place. "Nah. This place reminds me of the boiler room in *Nightmare on Elm Street*. Nothing new."

I kind of liked that.

We both moseyed up to the bar area of L'Amour. Melissa and I pressed up against the railing and kept talking. I noticed a couple of guys giving her the once-over, which filled me with something in the middle of fear, hatred, and flattery. I was angry that these guys were ogling my girl, flattered that I had a girl worth ogling, and scared of . . . what? Having her taken away from me? I didn't know. I decided to think about it. Brent's comments from earlier shot back into my brain for a split second, but I drove them off.

Melissa's voice yanked me back into consciousness.

"Sam, there's some guy watching you."

"What?"

"There's this guy who's looking at you. He's coming towards us. Do you know him?"

I turned around to have a lanky kid with bug eyes head-butt me in the stomach.

"Shane!" I pushed him back and gave him The Pound.

"Well, well, what have we he-ere?!" Shane said, imitating a detective discovering the final clue. "Last time I checked,

Sammy Markus was jus' too *kewel* for us metalhead kids! Wasn't that the case, Dan?"

Dan?! I looked up to see a larger kid, with a head full of frizzy hair and a goatee to match. "Now that you mention it, Shane," he said, nodding sarcastically with a mock-serious look on his face, "Sam *did* appear to be much too hip to spend a little time slumming it with us *despondent youth.*"

Death Metal Dan. Probably the coolest, nicest, smartest, funniest Malignancy fan I'd ever met. A legend in our own minds. The scene's equivalent to Fezziwig.

⬚⬚

I'd met Shane and Dan at my first L'Amour show, when they'd kept me from getting killed.

I was young, only about thirteen, and amazed at my first tiny club show. I'd never seen people like this before, and I'd sure as hell never seen anyone do to each other what these people were doing. I watched the mosh pit churn, with the fascination one has when passing a car wreck, inexplicably drawn to the violence swirling in front of me.

Since I'd never been to a show like this one, I had no idea what was allowed inside the club and what wasn't. I'd been given a basic pat-down on the way in, but they hadn't grabbed my wrists — both of which were adorned with spiked bracelets, hidden beneath the massive sleeves of my sweatshirt. I didn't know this would be a problem until one mosher got pushed a little too hard and crashed into me. Upon regaining his balance, we both saw that he'd torn his shirt and gotten a bright-red scratch down his chest. He grabbed my wrists and yelled, "What the fuck are *these*?" I was screwed.

But the minute the guy laid a hand on me, Dan pulled him off and tossed him back into the pit while Shane pulled me to safety. They calmed me down and let me know what was and wasn't cool to wear into a show. We spent the rest of the night talking about metal, and that was that. We didn't see each other that much outside of metal shows, but when we got together, it was clobbering time.

"I'm still too cool for the likes of you assholes," I said. "Shane, Dan, this is Melissa. Melissa, this is Shane and Death Metal Dan."

I always joked that Shane had "scene radar": He could immediately sense the kind of scene the person was involved in, especially whether or not it was *our* scene. I remembered it the minute he shook hands with Melissa. And as if on cue, he said, "AaaaHA! A tourist!"

"Sorry?" she asked.

"Is this your first metal show?"

Melissa stared in amazement, and then her slight surprise turned to annoyance. "Why do you wanna know? You want to pop my metal cherry or something?"

Jesus! When Melissa got nervous, she got tough!

"Well, it looks like Sam beat me to that!" he cackled. "I was just wondering because of the whole . . ."

As Shane worked his intuitive magic, Death Metal Dan put a hand on my shoulder. "She's puuuuurdy," he joked. "Nice catch, though. Seriously. How long've you been dating her?"

"Eh. About two months now, something like that."

"She's not very . . ."

"Metal?" I said, smirking.

"Exactly," he said.

"I know. I'm hoping to get her into it." After a pause, I muttered, "I dunno, man, I just like her more than I've liked a girl in a while."

"Congrats, my friend. Just be careful."

I looked up. "Why?"

Dan just shrugged. "A hunch, 's all. Just a feeling. Anyway," he said, tapping Shane upside the arm, "we're gonna go get a drink. We'll see you later. C'mon."

Shane and Dan stomped away. I turned to Melissa and said, "Those guys are great, aren't they?"

"Yeah. Yeah, they're cool, I guess."

"What? Why do you only guess?"

"They're nice and cool and all, just a little . . . bugged out, honestly. A little creepy."

I felt it right there for the first time. A pang. Pangs weirded me out in general, because I didn't like the idea of not being able to feel an entire emotion at once. Slivers of emotions weren't the most comforting idea to me. But a pang was what I got. A little pang of anger and resentment and bad feelings towards the one thing I adored in the world above all others. For a split second, the tiniest fraction of a moment, I was genuinely angry at her for saying that about my friends. It wasn't cool to judge. Why? Why'd she have to —

"Tell me more about this little club."

The feeling stopped. Forget it. She's wonderful. It's a great night. Don't fuck up.

Godsmack show, ninth grade. I'd promised Shane I would mosh for the first time. A lump of fear filled my throat, making it hard to breathe. Why had I told him I would do this? Everyone here was so much more hardcore than me. The bands on their T-shirts looked like the kind of people who kept their dead mother in their garage. Shane flanked me, laughing like a lunatic as some kid who'd been crowd surfing was tossed headfirst into a mosh pit, where his shoulder met the concrete floors.

"Shane, man," I said nervously, "I'm just a tiny bit antsy here."

He gave me a warm look and patted my shoulder. "Don't worry, Sam. You'll do fine." Then, looking back out into the pit, he mumbled, "Just keep those fists flying and those feet stomping." I shuddered. From where I was standing, this moshing business looked a lot like fighting.

"It looks like a brawl."

Shane stared off pensively, as if deciding how to respond to such a strange idea. He finally grabbed a good response, and his face lit up.

"Look," he yelled over Godsmack as they blared out groove-laden aggro onstage, "you know how ravers dance a certain way because the music is thumping and trippy? How the dance moves sort of imitate the music?"

I nodded. "Okay."

"And how, like, hippies noodle-dance?"

"Noodle-dance?"

"Yeah, y'know, they sort of wave their arms around and wiggle their bodies to go along with the music?"

"Okay, I know what you mean. What's your point?"

He motioned out to the center of the pit. "Moshing is just like that. It's not for the pain or to look tough or anything, it's just dancing that goes along with a certain type of music. In this case, it's incredibly violent, energetic dancing for violent, energetic music. You see?"

I sort of got it, and nodded to Shane. As our conversation ended, Godsmack began a new, extra-angry number. Suddenly, Shane's hand wrapped itself tightly around my forearm. I looked at him with a pleading face, begging to know what he was doing. Shane responded with a shit-eating grin.

"What — what are —"

"Let's dance!" he screamed.

Into the pit we leaped.

As I was explaining to Melissa why exactly a tiny nightclub in Brooklyn was one of the most important places in the world, the lights dimmed. The crowd went nuts, shrieking and howling, clearing a wide opening in the crowd for the pit. I reached down and gripped her arm involuntarily, pulling her down from the bar section and into the crowd. She looked up at me with a mixture of fright and excitement.

A shredding guitar chord broke through the silence. A red light faded slowly onto the room as smoke machines poured fog into the crowd. And there, in the center of the stage, wrapped in his bass, wearing his spiked anti-God armor, was Glen Benton. The man who had branded an inverted cross into his forehead. Like, seven times. The man who had single-handedly created satanic death metal. Glen Benton, Satan's lieutenant on Earth. Right on stage.

I nearly came.

He leaned forward and snarled into the microphone, "NEW YORK! GO FUCKING CRAZY! THIS SONG IS CALLED . . . 'BIBLE BASHER'!"

The first ripping guitar riffs of "Bible Basher" tore through the crowd, and the pit went insane. Leather-jacketed longhairs went flying, floor punching and windmilling all the way. A massively fat bald man in a shirt reading BEWARE OF GOD stomped through the pit, knocking kids down left and right.

"You ready?" I bellowed at Melissa, wrapping my arms around her waist.

"You want me to do THAT?!" she shouted, pointing at the pit.

"Yup!"

"No, Sam! No!"

"Yes, Melissa, YES!" I yelled and, pulling her tight, spun wildly into the controlled chaos ahead. We became a two-person top as I whipped her around in circles, her feet flying outwards with the centrifugal force and giving the dancers a good thrashing. I began whooping into her ear, my eyes wide and muscles taut. Soon, we'd almost cleared the pit, and she looked like she was having fun . . .

. . . until the fat bald guy slammed into us, the human equivalent of having a refrigerator chucked at our bodies. The sheer force of his huge, sweaty, agnostic belly hitting me blew my senses to hell. My hands opened, my grip fell apart, and I went flying. I turned in just enough time to see the floor rising up to give me a big ol' kiss.

Pain. Sharp pain. Funny, I didn't know my head could actually bounce off of the floor. I felt my skull hop once and then settle onto the wet ground with a sickening smack. My mind was a blur. What was going on? Ow. Deicide. Great song. OW. OOOOOW. Was she okay?

"TIME TO ADMIT YOU ARE SWIMMING IN FANTASY!"

Hands yanked me back to my feet. The room spun quickly. Calm down. Think. Look around. Was she okay?!

"BIBLE BASHER! BIBLE BASHER! BIBLE BASHER! WHO IS YOUR GOD?!"

Shane appeared at my side and yelled in my ear, "Dude, if you're lookin' for your woman, she's over there!"

He pointed towards the other side of the pit. She was pressed tight in the swishing crowd, being pushed repeatedly. Fuck. Mosh-pit logic: If someone goes into the pit, they want to be in the pit continuously. You don't leave a mosh very easily. I watched her being shoved and slammed, a look of utter despair on her face. No. She wasn't okay. *Get her out of the pit.*

And then the guy next to her, some skinny kid with the tips of his mushroom-cut dyed blue, leaned down and licked the side of her face.

⬜⬜

Okay, I'm not really all *that* violent. I've been in five real fights in my life, two of which resulted in me getting my ass handed to me. So I'm not too much a fighting guy. But that was my Melissa. The girl who I'd finally found, the one who I adored. And this kid, this fucking kid, he licked her, he smiled and licked the side of her face, and who the fuck did HE THINK HE WAS?!?!

▷

It happened fast. There wasn't any of that car-crash slow motion that you read about. It was fast and precise and cold. He *licked* her. *Licked her.* I simply shook off my daze, walked across the pit, reached over, and grabbed the kid by his stupid turquoise-tipped mushroom-cut, cradling the back of his head in my right palm.

"Hey, man, what the fuck?" he snarled, glaring at me.

I swung my left fist three times, each one connecting right in the center of his face. His nose bent a bad way. Blood began to spill wildly the minute the third punch landed. The kid made a small noise, stumbled backwards, and fell into the arms of his friend, a guy with dreads and a goatee. His buddy gaped at me, his face a mix of awe and rage.

"If you or Lumpy here come anywhere near me *or* her tonight," I said, pointing at him, my voice shaking and my hand hurting, spit flying from my mouth, "I will cripple you. *Cripple you*. Is that understood?"

Dread-boy gave me a short, amazed laugh, his mouth twitching.

"Get your friend some fucking Band-Aids."

I wrapped my arm around her shoulders. She huddled against me, wide-eyed, scared as hell. My other arm went out stiff and I shoved through the crowd like a linebacker, pulling her up the stairs leading to the bar. The crowd parted as we exited, one or two guys patting me on the back for my actions. When we finally got there, I used my shirt to wipe the remaining spit off her cheek.

"Are you okay?" I asked. "Oh my God, I'm so sorry, oh my God, I'm —"

I looked towards the stage. Deicide had just begun playing "Father Baker." Damn. I loved that song. I turned to her and said, "Look, you stay here and get some water, okay? I'm just gonna go back into the —"

"Take me home, Sam."

". . . What?"

"Home. Now. I want to go home." There was grief in her voice. Tears, almost.

I glanced at the stage.

"AT FATHER BAKER'S, YOU DO WHAT YOU'RE TOLD!"

"But, hon, there's —"

"Sam. Home. Now." She looked in my eyes. "Please."

I stared at her. Her face was set in stone. She was leaving, and either I was taking her home now or realizing what an idiot

I was later. I sighed, put my arm around her, and led her to the door.

We walked to the subway station in silence. The B train station at New Utrecht is aboveground, and lit by these endless fluorescent lights. From up on the platform you can see so much of Bay Ridge. I remember thinking of it as some sort of massive, illuminated insect towering above Brooklyn, keeping watch. You can't miss it, it's so bright and so high. I loved it. But tonight, there was only silence, with me and her clutched close together.

We sat there, waiting for the train to come, the empty track open before us like a huge metallic moat. I felt her head against my chest, her breathing still shaking. Slowly, I ran my hand through her long, brown hair.

"I've never seen that part of you before," she said.

I froze up. No. Oh, God, no.

"It was you, but full of . . . something." She buried herself deeper into me. "When you were moshing, you seemed alive and vibrant and . . . scary. When you hit that boy, you got even scarier. Like you became someone else. And I know this might sound horrible, but when I saw that other person . . . I wondered if that was the person I was dating. And when I thought it was, I wondered why. I wondered why someone like that had ever decided to be with me."

I ran my hands through her hair. "That wasn't me," I shushed, "that wasn't me. It was just an outburst. I'm not that person."

I felt her head shake. "Never again, Sam," she whispered. "I don't want to see that part of you. With those fists and those eyes and that face. You've never been like that before, and I don't want you to be like that again. Please."

I leaned my head down and kissed her. "Okay. Okay."

There was a pause. It felt like an eternity. And finally, I just managed to squeak out, "What . . . I mean . . . the other part of me, the part outside of the pit, what do you . . ."

I trailed off, looking away. Her head rose from my chest, and I felt a kiss softly planted onto my cheek. Her voice came, soft and tired and warm in my ear:

"I think I could love that part of you, Sam."

The train roared forward, and we boarded.

chapter 13

Don't Let 'Em Grind You Down

□□

I've always had this love of watching people when they don't know they're being watched. It's never been a sexual thing, which is the conclusion people inevitably jump to. I just like watching people in their own nature. Human nature is this brilliant, fascinating thing, and not many people admire it. Back in seventh grade, during my miserable-depressed-Goth period (*I'm so unloved, nobody understands, let's judge people*), I used to consider myself a misanthrope, but I don't think it's really that. I think I'm just enthralled by human nature, and that human nature is more often terrible than it is inspiring or admirable. That's why I love to watch people when they don't know about it: They don't feel the need to mask their true natures. I've seen people practice fight routines to themselves in crowded malls, recite complete Beatles albums while waiting for a bus, or pick their nose 'til it bled in the park (that guy was a businessman — his chin was totally scarlet by the end, as were his fingers). They become their real selves.

That Saturday on the subway ride to Brent's place, I watched this girl sitting a little ways away from me, across the aisle and down a few seats and a door. She wasn't doing anything special or weird — just reading a paperback mystery novel, her bags tucked between her legs. But she was so beautiful. She had chin-length dirty-blond hair, this slight chin, and these slender legs coming from under her khaki skirt. And I wondered if she knew I was looking at her, and whether or not she'd be offended. But mostly I just wondered if she knew how beautiful she looked. How utterly gorgeous she looked, right there in that seat. I don't think she saw me, but I knew right then that I'd remember her forever: this girl on the subway, totally oblivious to how utterly gorgeous she was while simply riding uptown.

Testament blared from my headphones as I walked off the train. The girl must've heard it, because she looked up with a slightly pissed look on her face. I smiled back at her. She ducked her head back into her paperback timidly. I sighed. Loud rock music equals bad kid equals don't make eye contact. She was so beautiful. I wondered what she'd say if I told her that.

"You're beautiful," I whispered.

If she heard me, she didn't respond. I walked out of the train, a little disappointed.

As I walked from the subway to Brent's house, I thought about last night. I didn't like the way Melissa saw me — if there was anyone I didn't want to intimidate, it was her. But most of all, the idea of having two sides bugged the living hell out of me, partly because I knew it was sort of true. I never consciously switched faces or anything; the situation just sometimes called for a different part of me to take over. Sometimes it was the part that could recite Edgar Allan Poe to Melissa while we lay in bed together, and other times it was the part that could do whiskey shots and listen to Quiet Riot.

I decided I should choose one or the other, and if I had to pick one, it would be the side Melissa wanted. She saw so much in that part of me. She said she could even love that part of me. And if that part of me could win the love of a girl like that, then it had to be the better half. Conan had to go and Sammy had to stay. Later, Mr. Hyde; hello, Dr. Jekyll.

Step one to being the new-and-improved boyfriend was to call her today. Melissa's parents were making her stay in and do homework, no visitors and no excursions allowed. I'd told her repeatedly that I would call her to keep her from stressing out and maybe even help her with her studying. She'd talked about how sweet it was of me, but it wasn't really that much trouble; I could talk with that girl for hours.

▷

I rounded the corner and walked towards Brent's place. He lived in a massive townhouse on the Upper East Side. We called it a cocaine addict's dream: white walls, gleaming banisters, clean rugs — you could snort a line off of the floor if you wanted to. Like the rest of us, his parents had a bit in their pockets, although they had a bit more than my folks or Irish's. We were comfortable. Brent was rich.

I met Deidre, his housekeeper, having a smoke outside.

"Hey, Deidre."

"Hey, Sam, how are ya?"

"Fine, thanks. You?"

"Eh, can't complain, can't complain. Looking for Brent?"

"Yeah, is he in?"

"Him and that red-haired kid just went out to get lunch. Should be back soon. Just go wait for him in his room, I'm sure he won't care."

"Aw, Deidre, you're a saint."

"Flattery'll get you nowhere, bub. Go on up."

I grinned at her, heading up to Brent's room. Deidre was the only thing that kept Brent in line. He wasn't a big fan of his parents, and no matter what they said, the boy wouldn't listen. Deidre, thankfully, didn't take any of his shit.

I climbed five flights of brilliantly polished stairs until I reached Brent's room, my little home away from home. (Brent joked that his parents would install an elevator, but then no one would *see* the stairs, and there's no point in having that many beautiful stairs if no one can stroke your ego about them.) We all slept, ate, hung out, whatever in Brent's room as if it were our very own, if only because he told us to. After checking my e-mail on his computer, I plopped down onto his bed (a mattress, blanket, and pillow on the floor) and waited.

"Incoming!"

A red-haired punk came flying at me at incredible speed. I put up my shields and raised the turret gun, but it was no use — I was bombed mercilessly. General, call the National Guard — the Irish has landed.

"OW! OW! OW!" he bellowed, rolling off of me. "SPIKES, dude! Fuck, you're like Indiana Jones's worst nightmare."

"Oh, darling. Love you, too."

"Damn straight. What's up?"

"Nothing, really. The usual. Earsplitting guitar riffs aaaaand being in love."

I looked up and saw Brent unpacking a grocery bag. "That's all you know, isn't it, you sad bastard? Romance and metal?"

"Don't you know it."

"Exactly," he scoffed. "I don't like hearing about your lovey-dovey schoolboy relationship, but having to hear about it with Testament in the background is just too much."

"You love it. What's in the bag?"

"Oh, yeah, baby. Lookie what we got," he said. Out of the bag came an eight-liter bottle of Coke, followed by a bottle of Jack Daniels. "Solid."

I felt myself tense up, about to try sobriety for the very first time. Well, actually, that was a lie — sobriety wasn't that hard for me. Telling my friends that I wasn't drinking . . . and doing so while resisting a tasty Jack-and-Coke . . . *that* would be a challenge.

"Pour me a big cup, dude," said Irish.

"Word. Three spiked sodas coming up."

"Make that two," I piped in meekly.

"What's up? You just don't feel like one?"

"Eh, yeah. And I'm giving up drinking."

I always thought that my friends simply wouldn't notice if I decided not to drink. Hell, I'd turned down a few over the years. But this was amazing. Everything froze, and four eyes immediately focused on my head in surprise and confusion. There was what felt like an eternity of silence. It was the one thing that I never actually believed would happen in this situation, and it was happening. *God dammit, guys*, I thought, *please don't do this.*

Brent broke the silence.

"Wait, what?"

"I'm not drinking anymore."

"Huh," Brent said blankly.

"No more drugs, either."

"Huh!"

Come clean. "Or smoking."

"Okay, now I'm gonna be nosy," said Irish, who was obviously amused. "What's the story, Conan?"

"Melissa's the story," Brent said. I sensed a little something in his voice. Not hurt. What? Worry. That was it. "She get you to go straightedge?"

"Oh, fuck you, Brent. It's not like that."

"She did. Thought so. Christ."

"This is my choice," I said slowly, liking the way the words felt. "This is something *I* want to do. *I* want to prove to myself that I can. So leave her alone, okay? She's not the issue."

I looked to Irish for support. He grinned and sang, "Dunna-nunna-nuh! Ka-rack that whip!"

"Girlfriend. I have. You don't."

Irish shrugged. "Okay. Whipped. You are. I'm not."

"Seriously, Sam," Brent said with a sigh. "I mean, just . . . seriously."

I could say that for Brent — when times got rough, he got profound.

"Look, what's the big deal, dammit? There's nothing wrong with going clean!"

"When you're trying to be something you're not, there is," mumbled Brent.

I glared at him. "The day I let my partying define *who I am* is the day I give up. I'm still the same person; I just don't drink or do drugs now, okay?" Brent kept shaking his head, and I decided a different tactic might work better. "It's not like my grades would be hurt by a little sobriety!"

"Oh, right, like that mattered before."

"I've got an idea. Let's change the subject, okay?"

"Fine," Brent said with a smirk. "How'd the concert go?"

Out of the frying pan and into the fire.

"It went . . ."

"Badly."

"It was fine."

"She was pissed off or disgusted or something of the like."

"It was going fine until some guy licked her. That was it."

"Told you so, man," he said.

"Look, when the music started and everything got going and that guy did what he did, I went nuts. Like I always do. And see-ing the look in her eyes, I realized that maybe that wasn't the kind of person I want to be. The concert went fine; I just decided that maybe I'm in for a change."

Brent looked at Irish, and Irish looked back at him, and then they both looked at me. It was like they were evaluating me, and it wasn't helping things. I began to wonder what they had been talking about on their trip to the liquor store before I arrived.

"So how about you either let me in on the little inside joke between you two," I growled, "or you stop all of this judgmental bullshit and leave me alone?"

Everyone went silent. I glowered at Brent, who stared casually back at me. I hated that about him. No matter how angry I was at him, he would just stare at me with a look that read, *Well, what do you want me to do?*

Irish glanced back and forth between us, finally gulping down his drink and breaking the silence with, "SO! When's the movie?"

"Oh, yeah," said Brent, taking a slug from his drink, "we're seeing *The Dark Fantastic* in about an hour. It's a horror flick. You wanna come?"

I shrugged. "If it's over by three."

"Why?"

"I have to be home by three-thirty."

Irish looked confused. "That early? Why?"

"I have to call . . . someone."

Silence again. My attempt at a cover-up was worthless. They knew who I was calling.

Brent heaved a sigh and shook his head. "Dude," he said, "I think she can deal."

I glanced at Irish and then at Brent. Both of them had the

same sort of face on: disappointed. And when I thought about it, I was a little disappointed, too. Maybe this wasn't just a way for them to torment me. Perhaps they actually wanted me to spend some time with them. They'd just picked one hell of a frustrating way to tell me that, the bastards.

"Okay, fuck it. Let's go see the movie," I mumbled. I was not going to let them win.

"Solid," Brent said. "It's at two. The theater on 86th and Lex."

Irish whispered something about leashes not stretching that far. I hit him in the stomach.

chapter 14
Head Like a Hole

▷

We hung out around Brent's place for a while longer, him and Irish shooting the shit while I stayed silent. By then, I didn't even want to go to the damn movie, but I was determined to show them that it was my choice to change, not hers. I was under no one's control but my own.

But my front fell apart quickly. As we walked to the movie, and as we sat in the theater, I just felt myself falling back into rhythm with them. The dirty jokes started flying, and we became the sophomoric teenagers we always were with each other.

The previews were a slaughterhouse.

"A *car commercial*?! I have a TV at home for this crap!"

"Oh, look! His cell phone went off in the theater and they hit him for it! That's so funny and original and hip! Shoot me."

"Yeah, I'll Fan your Dango any day, sweetie pie!"

"A Rob Schneider movie where he acts like an idiot and gets the girl for it?! BRILLIANT! OSCAR!"

"That movie looks about as fun as a Coldplay album."

And so on. The movie itself was a riot. Between zombies pulling the head off of a priest who's trying to battle them with a massive cross and a demonically possessed businessman calling down a giant demon to attack a scantily clad, big-boobed teen star, we had a blast. The rest of the moviegoers weren't all that happy about our behavior, but to hell with 'em. By the time we stood up to go, all issues were forgotten, and we were friends again.

"Best. Movie. Ever," said Brent, shaking his head.

"Dude, when the evil choirboys started vomiting blood." I shook my head. "That right there was classic cinema."

"I know!" yelled Irish. "Or, like, when the guy opened the confessional booth, and —"

"THE ZOMBIES LEAPED OUT AND ATE HIM!" we cackled simultaneously. These were the kind of days I lived for: horror movies with friends. The whole drinking-smoking-partying thing was fun. And, yeah, shows were really, really great. But my favorite times always seemed to be the ones where it was just me, a couple of friends, and a stack of scary movies.

But then it happened. As we began walking out of the theater's glass doors, my shoulder managed to collide with that of some girl getting off of the snack line, spilling her popcorn and sending her Raisinets tumbling to the ground. I really hate doing that — I never tried to be tough when I bumped into people; I was just clumsy. I whipped around and said, "Oh, wow, dude, I'm totally sorry."

Standing there was a girl in a sweater vest and thick black

glasses, her bag covered in stitched-on band patches and buttons reading things like AND YOU'RE TELLING ME THIS BECAUSE . . . ? Standing next to her was a girl with frizzy red hair and glasses that weren't thick and black like her friend's, but made up for it in lens diameter. She was wearing a red shirt with a biohazard symbol on it, a denim beret, and blue-and-white flare pants. The one in the sweater vest picked up her candy and said, "How about you watch where you're going, *dude*?"

"I'm . . . I said I was —"

"Oh, no, no, it's hella-fine, *bro*," said the redhead, putting her hands out. "We're wicked good."

□□

Oh my fucking GOD. *Hipsters*.

I'd met these kids all over the place. These are the kids who are *so* sure that they're *so* ahead of everyone else, and that they're *so* much more intelligent than most other people because of their music choice. You know one of these kids, I bet. Y'know, the kid who thinks because they like Brainiac or the Specials instead of KISS or Jay-Z, they're the great minds of their generation. I've always thought that, as much as I utterly loathed some of it, music was still music, be it Annihilator or Good Charlotte or Ja Rule or Sigur Rós or Christina fucking Aguilera, and that assholes are assholes, regardless of their musical taste. Hipsters, though, were the anti-what-I-just-said. There are hipsters for every musical genre: metal hipsters, Goth hipsters, rap hipsters, even country hipsters (well, a few). And by the look of it, I had two emo/indie megahipsters in front of me — the worst kind. I don't know why, but it just seemed like those two genres of music bred more hipsters than any other.

▷

I was about to flip out. My blood boiled in my head. My ears felt like they had fire ants inside of them. *Don't let that side out,* I told myself. *Don't let that side out! You're more than that!*

Thank God, though: Brent and Irish had no such desire to restrain.

"Hey, fuck you, you hipster trash!" snarled Irish, throwing up a stern middle finger.

"I think I hear a Sk8er Boi calling in the next room," cackled Brent, flipping the girls an equally stern bird. "How about you go wax existentialism with him, you screaming infidelity skanks?!"

"Hurry!" laughed Irish. "He might start crying otherwise!"

And me? I just smiled, waved, and said, "Bye, ladies."

"Ugh," scoffed Sweater Vest, stomping away.

And that was why I loved my friends. Because when it all came down to it, they shared the same Holden Caulfield ideals that I did: Live how you want, feel how you feel, and fuck all the phonies in your way.

I said my good-byes, giving each of them The Pound and a pat on the back. I hailed a cab on 86th Street and got back around four-thirty, bounding upstairs towards my room happily with Slipknot under my breath. On my way up, Erica poked her head out of her room.

"Melissa called."

I paused. "How do you know her name?"

She stepped out now, her little preppy self with Destiny's Child in the background. "She told me," she said. "I talked to her for a little bit. She called, like, five times. Sounded kind of distressed."

"No big deal," I said, shrugging. "Just wants to talk to me."

My sister shrugged back. "Okay. Just . . . y'know."

"You know what?"

"Nothing."

"No. Wait. You can't do that. Tell me."

"Just don't get stuck with a . . . *drama* girl." She turned around and was swallowed by the pink once more.

I shuffled into my room all in a huff (oh, yes, as much as we'd like to think otherwise, us heterosexual males do get in huffs now and again), the words Brent and Irish had said earlier that day echoing in my burning ears. Why the hell was everybody climbing all over Melissa? I hated it. I hated how everyone, including a thirteen-year-old Britney Spears fan, suddenly thought they knew everything about this girl. On top of it, they thought that the everything was just me being ordered around. It wasn't like that. They didn't understand that feeling I got when it was just me and her . . . like there was nothing else in the world that really mattered but her, there, staring into my eyes and smiling. Talking music with me. Talking philosophy with me. Talking anything with me. Hell, last week, we lay in her bed and discussed which Greek gods we wanted to be ("Artemis? You want to be a god*dess*? That's so cool!"). They didn't know.

First things first, I slipped Megadeth's *Peace Sells . . . But Who's Buying?* into my stereo. Then I grabbed the phone and punched her number into it as quickly as humanly possible. There were two rings before it got picked up.

"Sam?"

"Hey, yeah, it's me."

"Where the hell were you?"

Venom. Not the band. Pure venom in her voice. Like, hissing, angry, reptilian poison spat at me from an open mouth. I sank down to my floor, mouth agape, trying to think of something, anything, that I could say to her. She read my silence and went on.

"I wanted to talk to you so much, Sam, and you weren't there. You weren't there when *you* said that *you* would call *me*. What happened?"

"I just went out to a movie with friends," I managed to sputter out.

"Oh, great." She sighed. "That's nice. I could've gotten work done for the last hour or so, but instead I put it all aside so it wouldn't cut into our talking time. The time that *you* so *adamantly* promised we would have to talk."

Another pang. Snap, zing, boom, snikt. Why was she yelling at me? This wasn't fair. It's not like I cheated on her or forgot her birthday or hurt her cat. I'd just missed a phone call because I was having fun with a couple of my friends. She couldn't just — Wait. Stop. Think, man, think. Think about Greek gods, how she wanted to be Demeter and you wanted to be Artemis. Think about her breath mixing with yours, and the way her belly skin felt when your fingers ran along it, and her lips, that soft press followed by that sticky, grasping pull, as if your lips were trying their best to stay together. Her soft voice, her quick wit, her brilliant skin. You in a ball on her couch. Think of all the wonderful, beautiful things she's brought to your life, and hold it. Grip it. Keep it there. Do not be the Fuck-Up. Now, you may speak.

"I'm so sorry," I managed. "Time just got away from me. I shouldn't have promised you I'd call if there was a chance I might not, or I should've called you to let you know I'd call you back later. I'm sorry."

There were what seemed like a few minutes of dead air, until I heard her say, "Who were you with?"

"Irish and Brent."

"Huh. Figures."

Wait, what? "What's that supposed to mean?"

"Just that those two aren't exactly responsible people and all."

"Well, I mean, c'mon, dear . . ."

"The one nearly puked on my shoes! I dunno, they just seem a little crazy and immature."

I said, "Yeah, I know," in a sort of funny, *aw-shucks* manner, as if I were shamefully proud of my crazy friends. I sounded harmless.

I felt deadly.

I wanted to break something.

"By the way," she said, "if there are no other movies playing" (pang: I said I was sorry) "could you not make any plans for a week from this Friday and Saturday?"

"Um, sure. What's going on that Saturday?"

"I want you to have dinner with my friends. I thought, you got to submit me to your world" (pang: word choice . . . *submit*

107

you?) "so now it's my turn to bring you into mine, which, trust me, is a lot less violent." (pang: Didn't *you* ask *me* if you could come to the show?) "Is that okay?"

Don't be the Fuck-Up. "Yeah, sure. What's Friday?"

"That," she said conspiratorially, "is a secret, my love."

"Ooooh," I mocked. "I'm itching to know."

"Patience, my dear. I'll leave it to your imagination."

My imagination went fucking nuts, immediately pumping blood to what de Sade would've called my "lower extremities."

"And you're *sure* you can make those days?"

"I will tattoo them onto my forehead, ma'am. I promise."

"Okay. Sorry if I'm being a little drastic, I just really wanted to talk to you, and it worried me when you didn't call."

"Understood. I'm sorry."

"So, what movie was so good that it took the place of my call?"

"*The Dark Fantastic.*"

"Pffff. Figures."

Pang.

chapter 15
Cruelty and the Beast

▷

Me and Irish walked down the hall that Wednesday, shaking our heads as we exited pre-calc. There'd been a pop quiz. A pop quiz in pre-calc was like coming home to find out your mother has thrown out all your old issues of *Revolver* because they were "taking up room."

I glanced at Irish. "Did you get that one with the two roads and the train?"

He shook his head. "Man, I don't want to talk about it."

I thought for a second. "Which problem made you hit your head against the desk like that?"

"I *said*," groaned Irish, "that I don't want to talk about it." He looked up at me and half smiled. "Manhattan Diner?"

"Waffles."

"Damn straight," he said, readjusting one of his bag straps.

We hurried towards the door, talking about how much we

hated our teacher and how much we hated life. As we headed past the mailroom where the student mailboxes were kept, a voice yelled out, "Hey, Markus!"

I turned and looked. There stood Mickey Brock, a sophomore with a huge mouth and no respect for his elders. He had a big, stupid smile on his face, and was surrounded by a small crew of toadies. "Why don't you wear black nail polish?"

I stared at him for a moment. "Um . . . should I be wearing it?"

"It's just," he laughed, "all the Goths at my summer camp did that, so I thought it was, like, standard uniform . . ."

The hair went up on the back of my neck. My eyes filled up with blood. My spine seemed to clench together, making my entire body go tense and stiff. Next to me, I saw Irish's eyes widen and heard him say, "Ooooh, shit . . . OOOOOH, shit . . ."

"Did . . ." I hissed at Brock slowly, "did you just call me a *Goth*?"

Brock glanced around with a *Pfff, what's wrong with* this *guy* look and said, "Uh, yeah . . . you *are* a Goth, aren't you? I mean, look at you."

I smiled. Just a little bit. A smirk more than a true smile. Slowly, I advanced towards him.

"I get it, okay. Black clothes, combat boots, spiked bracelets, all that, that means I'm a Goth. You've seen Chris Kattan on *SNL* doing the Goth Talk skit, and he looked a little like me, so you figure I'm a Goth."

I was now only a few feet away from him, his smile shortening along with the distance between us.

"So, the question is, where are my Bauhaus CDs, huh? Where's my face powder and my fishnet shirt? I mean, I don't see any steel-claw attachments on my fingers, and . . . wait . . . no, I don't think I'm wearing any fake fangs or eye shadow. I don't *appear* to have a single fucking ruffle on my clothing, and my jacket, coincidentally, is not made of fucking lace, velvet, *or* satin! NO makeup! NO contacts! At all!"

I had him pressed against a wall now, my face only inches from his chubby, quivering one. His toadies had all backed off to one side of the room or the other.

"Let me tell you two things, Mickey," I growled. "First is that if wearing black nail polish is 'standard uniform,' then I guess I'm just even more of a rebel by *not* wearing it, right?"

"Geez, Markus, I was only —"

"RIGHT?!"

He gulped. "Right."

"Right. Secondly, I think you've already gotten the point, but just to make it extra clear, I'm going to nail it through that big! thick! fat! skull of yours, okay? So, here it is, just to get this down: I AM NOT A FUCKING GOTH. I'M A METAL-HEAD. THEY ARE NOT THE SAME THING. It's a Venn diagram solution, really, you see? You know what a Venn diagram is? It's one of those math problems with two or three intersecting circles that sometimes end up looking like Mickey Mouse's head. Y'see, you fat-headed weasel, some metalheads ARE Goths, and some Goths ARE metalheads. They are not mutually exclusive, but they are not always connected. So let's repeat: What did we learn today?"

Brock gulped again. "You're not a Goth?"

"What am I?"

"A metalhead. Just a metalhead."

I patted his chubby cheek. "There's hope for you yet,

Brock." Turning to exit, I mumbled, "C'mon, Irish, I need some fucking waffles."

Irish couldn't stop cackling, clutching his stomach, and leaping mindlessly around the halls. "'Math problems with Mickey Mouse's head?' Jesus, man, that was depraved!"

I grunted. "Piss off. It made me angry."

"Yeah, I noticed! Christ, that kid's gonna have a complex now!"

"Shut up."

"What do you have against Goths, anyway?"

"Nothing. I have a lot of Goth friends. I'm just *not* one. It's an ignorant label, is all."

"Geez, someone's a little testy . . ." Irish chuckled.

"Well, what about you that day those girls at that party called you *Avril-y*?"

He stopped laughing. "Completely different situation."

We turned the corner to exit school and I stopped dead. Melissa was leaning against the door, looking around expectantly. I glanced at Irish, who in turn glanced back at me. We didn't say a word, just walked out together slowly.

Her eyes caught me and she whipped around. "Hey!" she called, and leaped into my arms. I grasped her, giving her a kiss on the neck and never taking my eyes off of Irish.

"What are you doing here?"

"Oh, I was in the neighborhood, so I thought I'd, y'know, surprise you. Maybe get coffee?"

I shot one at Irish. "Uuuuh . . ."

He simply nodded and walked away.

". . . yeah. Yeah, I guess coffee would be great."

She glanced at his back. "Does he want to come along?"
I shrugged. "Apparently not."

Now, what the hell was that all about, Irish?

We ended up at the Starbucks on 81st and Broadway. Now, let me make something clear: I have no problem with Starbucks. Everyone I know has some sort of issue against Starbucks, that it's, I dunno, too corporate, a tool of the system, yadda yadda yadda. In the metal scene, being seen with a cup of Starbucks coffee is like saying you *like* the new direction Metallica is going in. I don't really get it, personally. If the system makes quality coffee, well, hail the system. It wasn't Manhattan Diner, but it was okay.

As I slurped my caramel icy thingy and she had her no-foam mocha thingy, she said, "So what exactly *are* Brent and Irish on the friend spectrum?"

The whozza? "What do you mean?"

"Well, I mean, are they your *best* friends or, like, just your guy friends?"

I shrugged. "They're my guy friends who are my best friends."

"Aaaaah," she said, nodding slowly, "I get it." That made one of us. "So, like, what do you guys *do*?"

What was with this strange line of vague-but-probably-very-meaningful questioning? "We hang out. Go out to eat. Talk. Go to the movies. Listen to music a lot. Get wasted —" She looked up at me sternly and I smiled sheepishly. "— or so we *used* to, before my life was miraculously turned around."

She grinned and said, "Yay." But then the grin was gone and she became thoughtful. "But, I mean, like . . . me and my friends, we get together to hang out, sure. But, like, we'll be doing something. Going to the Met or making fondue or something. That's what I mean."

I shrugged again. "I mean . . . sure, sometimes we *end up* doing something, but, y'know . . . when we get together to hang out, we don't really have a plan. We just hang out. Usually, we just . . . keep doing that."

She nodded again and said, "Ah."

And that "Ah," man. Maybe I was reading into it, but that "Ah" had something to say. It had a million meanings behind it, with everything from "Sounds fine" to "So, you're basically just a bunch of no-good slacker stereo monkeys, then." And suddenly I had all those meanings in my head at once, and they came together, and they formed one big PANG.

So I thought I'd try it out. I'd been considering it for a while now, and all I needed was a chance to try it out. I was going to ask her. I was going to come clean.

"Am . . . am I, like, good enough for you? Am I okay?"

She looked up at me with alarm, which made me a *little* happier. "Yes, of course, hon. Why do you ask?"

"Well, it's just, like, you've been trying to change me, is all. Like, getting me to go straightedge, aaaand, I dunno, what you said after the concert about seeing a certain side of me . . . I dunno. Do you even *like* me?"

She leaned across the table and kissed me hard, like she was trying to prove something. She ran her hand through the hair on the back of my head, shoved her tongue in my mouth, the whole deal. I was just shocked.

Then she leaned back and answered me straight, without a hint of sarcasm or pity in her voice. "I feel like this, Sammy," she said. "I feel like . . . like you have this, this amazing *potential*, basically. Like, you *can* be this bright, amazing human being when you want to be, but that there are these things that set you back. I think booze and drugs might be some of 'em. I think the violence and attitude thing might be another two. To be honest, I actually think Brent and Irish might also be in there. Even, I dunno, your *obsession* with heavy metal. Sometimes it seems like you even fall into that caricature you hate so much. I just feel like you have the potential to shine, to light up the darkness in you with who you are. And I want to see that shine. I want to see that side of you blossom and become what I think it can. I think there're times when you hinder *yourself*. I'm just trying to be . . . I dunno, a catalyst."

This was confusing. On the one hand, I hadn't heard the word "potential" said that many times about me since my last parent–teacher conference. But on the other hand, my heart had never felt quite so warmed by something as it did now. She saw something in me, and she wanted to make it grow, to make me better. She wanted my light to throw out the darkness in me. I couldn't think of anyone who cared about me like that, other than my parents. And that felt incredible. To be able to inspire someone to care *that* much about you. Jesus, that was like "Angel of Death" in the front row, like "Enter Sandman" coming on the radio while you're driving with your friends. That was perfect.

I reached for my little paper Starbucks cup and lifted it slightly in the air, saying, "A toast, then."

She raised hers, bemused. "To what?"

"To blossoming."

I'd drink to that.

chapter 16
This Love

▷

Friday Friday Friday Friday Friday calm the fuck down Friday Friday.

I knocked on her apartment door, quickly checking myself over. Did I have everything? Did I do everything right? Deodorant. Check. Brushed teeth. Check. Brain. Eh. Okay. I was okay for whatever would come to me.

And she came to me, in a wonderfully tight tank top and a pair of hip-huggers. A little glitter lined her eyes, and something glossy and wet-looking ran along her lips.

"Why, hello there," she purred softly.

I tried to speak, but suddenly realized I'd forgotten English. Words finally pieced themselves together in my head and forced their way through all the testosterone floating around in my brain before finally reaching my vocal cords.

"You look gorgeous."

"Thank you, my darling. You don't look too shabby yourself." She smiled. "Come on in. Popcorn's just finished popping."

I walked in to face Mr. and Mrs. Andrews, Melissa's parents. Things slowed down in a flash of disappointment: Her parents were here. Not only that, but this was to be my first meeting with them. A thought flew through my head reminiscent of 1930s detective noir: She'd set me up, dammit. I had expected an evening alone and uninterrupted, but no. This was apparently a night in — with the fam, no less.

"Ah, the great Samuel," said her father in a deep, Canadian Mountie voice. He was a big tree of a man with a broad, shiny forehead and brown hair creeping around the sides. Old-fashioned spectacles sat on the bridge of his nose, and a couple of faux-marble pens jutted out of his shirt pocket. A hand thrust out before me, sleeved in a blue oxford shirt, with a Yale ring on one finger.

I took his hand, giving it a firm, quick shake (for dads, handshakes matter . . . a lot). "Pleasure to finally meet you, too, sir."

A warm smile came over his thin lips. "Good handshake. I like this boy already."

Score.

Next came Mom, a thin, wiry woman of my height with a massive, toothy smile outlined in red. Brown hair tumbled down to about her chin, and the hand she offered gracefully to me was thin and bony. I shook it with both hands (handshakes for mothers require both hands, of course), and heard her say what I was hoping she would:

"We've heard so much about you!"

Double score. Time for Charming Boyfriend Routine #7:

ME: (*embarrassed glance at Melissa*) Uh-oh. You have?

MOM: (*fling of hand*) Oh, all good of course. All good.

DAD: (*hearty chuckle*)

ME: I only wish I could believe you, Mrs. Andrews, oooor Ms. Andrews, oooor . . . I'm never quite sure how polite I should be.

MOM: Oh, please, dear, *Tracy and Richard* is fine. And yes, we've heard so many good things about you. Melissa just doesn't stop talking about you.

ME: Oh, no, now you have expectations! I'm going to be a letdown!

DAD: (*hearty chuckle*)

MOM: Oh, please. I'm *sure* you'll live up to the hype.

ME: (*loving, romantic glance at Melissa*) Well, I'll do my darnedest.

MOM: So, Samuel, you go to a pretty prestigious school — how does that suit you?

ME: Oh, it was scary at first, but you can't help but love it, Ms. — I mean, Tracy.

MOM: That school has quite a reputation going for it! What's that like?

ME: Well, it's a really competitive environment, but it's also incredibly rewarding. I'm having a great time.

DAD: (*knowing nod*)

MOM: That's wonderful. Isn't that wonderful, sweety?

DAD: (*energetic nod*) Rmm-hmm.

MOM: Now, what's it like being in an all-boys school?

ME: Oh, you really don't mind after a while. When you do things like theater and whatnot like I do, you meet enough girls that you can really have a very healthy social life.

MOM: Well, obviously. I mean, that's how you met our little girl, yes?

ME: (*wistful laugh*) Exactly! I take one acting assignment
and end up with a girlfriend! It honestly couldn't have
worked out better. A dream come true.

⬜⬜

Call me a sellout all you fucking want, but the Charming
Boyfriend Routine was key to existence. Even if your significant
other had monsters for parents, life was a whole lot easier when
those monsters actually let you see her. On top of that, the way
I dressed and the music I listened to made me an easy target for
parental attacks; the inconsistency of showing them I was a
sweet, eloquent young man was just too much.

I'd learned the art subtly from my older brother's girlfriends.
The first time he brought a girl home, she proceeded to
become my mother's best friend in a matter of minutes. I was
floored. I couldn't talk my way out of a B+ with the woman, and
here was a teenager with a craftily constructed persona who
was winning her over. When I asked her how she did it, she
shrugged and said she just read the parents' appearance and
told them what they wanted to hear. I thought that was
amazing. For years, the Charming Boyfriend and Charming
Girlfriend routines were the only times I tolerated anyone
being blatantly plastic in public.

You get the idea. After a couple minutes more of this, with Melissa spying nervously onward from the sides, I was given the best news of the night: Her mom and dad were departing for the theater. They were leaving us to our own devices, although I had to be out of the house by eleven, and there was to be no bad behavior while they were gone, is that understood, which of course it enthusiastically was.

I smiled politely and told them it was nice meeting them. They shook hands with me again (this time, Richard was ready, and nearly turned my carpals to silt), and slowly filed out of the door. As they were entering the elevator, Mrs. Andrews laughed out, "And don't scratch up the furniture with those spikes!"

Ha. Ha ha. Funny lady.

The door clicked shut softly, and I was left to face the most wonderful brunette Shakespeare obsessive in the world.

She shook her head. "That was amazing. I cannot *believe* the sheer amount of bullshit that just came out of your mouth."

I went to her and wrapped my arms around her waist. "Master thespian, dear. May I?"

We kissed. Deeply. A suggestive kiss. A kiss not to be given around adults.

"Come on," she whispered. "*Zoolander* awaits."

Ceiling fans. I wondered who came up with the idea for ceiling fans. I found them utterly hypnotic. I didn't have one in my room and always kind of wished that I did. They were so . . . classy. So retro. A ceiling fan gave a room a certain kind of atmosphere. They had personality. I loved personality.

I felt shifting in the sheets next to me and a hand rub against my arm. From the corner of my eye, I caught a mop of dyed-red hair move over and perch on my shoulder, nuzzling up against me.

"Whatcha' thinking about?" Mina asked, stretching like a house cat in the sun.

"Ceiling fans," I said softly, pulling my eyes away from the twirling marvel hanging above me. I pulled my arm out from the sheets next to me and put it around her bare shoulders.

". . . Ceiling fans?"

"Yeah, ceiling fans. I like them. Don't you?"

She shifted again. "Mmm. I never really . . . I don't know. They're just ceiling fans."

I nodded and looked back up at the fan spinning above us. Slowly but surely, I became aware. Aware of the silence in the room, of the thinness of the sheets, of my nakedness in someone else's bed.

She put her hand on my chest and rubbed it back and forth, making a little kitty noise in her throat. I would've found it really hot at any other time.

Huh, I thought. *I really wish we hadn't done that.*

We spent the next half hour pretending to watch Ben Stiller make stupid puckering faces. I liked the movie, sure, and warm popcorn with a beautiful girl is always nice, but there was something up. Melissa kept glancing at me, smiling slightly, and I gave her back nervous little stares, frowning worriedly. Finally, after maybe forty-five minutes of movie, she looked straight at me and said, "Tell me about your romantic past."

Something inside of my brain went on total defense mode. "Why do you want to know about my romantic past?"

She shrugged. "I dunno. Just wondering. Why are you being so defensive?"

"I'm not being defensive. *You're* being defensive. What about *your* romantic past?"

"Oh, come on!"

"Okay, seriously." I sighed. "Why do you want to know about that?"

A second shrug. "I just think it's relevant, is all."

I gave her the once-over. She was beautiful. She was fun. She had been a wonderful girlfriend to me. And I trusted her.

"Okay," I said. "Here goes . . ."

Out spilled the beans. I told her about Alex, my first girlfriend, who'd described me as "sad" after we broke up.

About Ivy, my second girlfriend, who dumped me after only a month of dating but still managed to rip my heart to shreds, the only ex-girlfriend I was still really good friends with out of the whole list.

About Tonya, who I'd met at camp and totally adored, but who lived in Maine.

About Lacey, the girl I dated who had carved my name into her ankle and wanted me to do the same for her.

And about Mina, the Goth girl I had dated previous to Melissa, a relationship that had turned out disastrously.

"She broke up with her boyfriend to be with me," I said, "and I dumped her after a few months. I just wasn't . . . compatible with her. We didn't talk about much else but music and sex, and it got really, really boring after a while."

"Why'd you date her in the first place?"

"Her name."

"Her name?!"

I grinned sheepishly. "Ever read *Dracula*?"

Melissa stared at me in amused horror. "You dated a girl because she shared the same name as a character in *Dracula*?!"

"I know. It was stupid. She was a Goth and all, and I guess I sort of saw myself as the Dark Prince character, and I was stealing her from her stupid human boyfriend, and . . . yeah."

"That's the dumbest thing I have ever heard. Ever."

"Yeah, me, too."

"Are you a virgin?"

Gut-wrenching question number two.

"No."

Her eyebrows went up. "Oh, really?"

I nodded. "Mina was my first. We were really attracted to each other." Then, thinking it through, I asked, "Are you?"

She nodded. "Just . . . haven't found the right guy yet. Or maybe I have."

"Sorry?"

"So now there's me," she said.

"Yes," I answered, though she hadn't really asked a question. "Now there's you."

"C'mere," she whispered, and slid across the couch to me.

I wrapped myself around her and kissed her. Just like before: a kiss that suggested something. She threw a knee over my legs and straddled me, pushing me down into the couch with her kisses. My eyes closed, and my body responded to touch. Hands sliding up my chest. My fingers curling around her neck. Flinging my spikes off of my wrists and burying my lips into her neck. The smell of her hair. Her breath on my ear, hot, quick, powerful.

Her shirt went over her head, a movement that surprised me, but in the best possible way. My hands studied the intricacies of her back, her stomach, her neck. A bra strap fell down from its perch on a shoulder, and I immediately kissed the warm skin underneath. My lips moved softly down, from shoulder to collarbone, from collarbone to breast. I felt my skin prickle and my muscles grow taut, and right then reality existed only in the places where our flesh touched.

I felt a lip brush against my earlobe, sending electric shocks through my body. Her voice came out ragged, quickly, frantically.

"Make love to me, Sam."

I froze up. I didn't fall from my heat-of-the-moment grace — it simply ceased to exist. My hands, my lips, my entire body sat in a fixed position. The real world came flying back to me with all the gentleness of a cactus to the tailbone.

"What?" I whispered.

"Right now. Make love to me."

And worst of all, the things I wanted least in this moment — my conscience, my morals, my code, my sense of responsibility — all confronted me and refused to budge. All of a sudden, I wasn't thinking about being naked and happy with the girl I adored — I was thinking about what this would mean for us. How things would change. And in a split second, Instinct lost to Reason, and I said a word I hated the minute I heard it.

". . . no."

Now it was Melissa's turn to freeze. Her voice broke its husky whisper and came out confused and upset. "What?"

"No."

"What do you mean, no?"

I was getting frustrated. "You heard me. No. What else *could* I mean?"

She sat up and looked at me with what could only be anger. "Why not?"

"We've only been dating two months or so," I sputtered, "and while I totally would like to, I don't really think —"

"You slept with this . . . this Dracula girl!"

Wait, what? Was that why she wanted to know about my romantic life?

"Exactly," I said, my brain operating at full speed again. "And my first time is something that, quite honestly, I don't want to remember. I'd prefer to remember yours in a different light."

"Oh, so this," she said in an ugly voice, "this is because you care about me?"

"Yeah. Basically."

And that was all it took. She climbed off of me, mumbling something under her breath, yanking her tank top on viciously. Finally, she plopped down as far away from me as humanly possible on the couch, shaking her head and staring stubbornly at the movie.

"Oh, Melissa . . ." I said through clenched teeth, "please . . ."

"You know, this is the first case I've ever heard of the *guy* not being ready. Your machismo wears off pretty quickly, huh?"

Ow. My manhood ached. What the hell was wrong with me? A beautiful girl who I was heels-over-head crazy about just offered me consensual sexual intercourse — and I was turning it down?! Why? Why couldn't I just switch my morals off and go for the gold? Whatever happened to all the heavy-metal tough-guy bullshit I'd so adamantly banged my head to? Whatever happened to womanizing and domination and kinkiness? What the fuck was *wrong with me*?

"Well . . . thanks," I mumbled, rising. "Guess I'll be going now."

"No. Sam. Wait."

I sat back down, facing her. She had her head propped up with one hand, and an upset look on her face. "I'm really . . . I'm really, really sorry. I had this plan . . . this idea. And it didn't work out. I just . . ."

"Thought it would be perfect."

"Right."

"I'm sorry."

"Oh, hey" — she looked up at me — "you shouldn't be. It's not your fault. You're actually . . . the one thinking here. You're right. I'm going too fast for my own good."

I looked down at the carpet, saying nothing. I heard a slow rustling of cushions and clothes, and then a hand cradling my cheek.

"Honey?"

"Yeah," I said, looking into her pleading eyes. "I just . . . my ego isn't doing too well right now. . . ."

"Shhhh. I'm sorry."

She leaned in and kissed me. Not like all of the other kisses tonight; a genuine, heartfelt kiss. I put my arms around her waist and pulled her close to me, clutching her like a kid with his security blanket.

"I wish I could be the guy you want," I said.

"You are," she whispered, placing her head against my chest. "You're exactly the guy I want."

We lay there on her couch, listening to each other breathe, until the sound of a key in the lock split us apart.

chapter 17
The Beautiful People

Saturday night. My mom was fucking ecstatic. "You're wearing a collared shirt outside of school? I *must* meet this girl!"

"Yeah, well, you'll get to. She's coming to pick me up."

Mom's eyes went huge and a grin — a real grin — crept across her face. "Yeah? I'm looking forward to it."

"Indeed. Now, if you don't mind too much, could I have some privacy?"

"Right away, sir," she said, then exited my bedroom, closing the door behind her.

Dress nicely — that's what Melissa had told me. We were apparently meeting her friends in a rather posh place for dinner or drinks or something, a place that wasn't exactly accepting of the band-T-shirt-and-ripped-jeans look. With that said, I was simultaneously giving my mom a dream and myself a nightmare.

I was actually going to wear my school clothes outside of school. Blue collared shirt, slacks, and a tie.

I looked at myself in the mirror. Okay . . . I looked like a simp, sure, but a decently dressed simp. I strolled over to my closet and got out the finishing touch to my outfit.

I'm not quite sure how or why bullet belts became popular in metal fashion. I suppose it was simply the insanity value — people in strange-looking clothes with strings of artillery strapped across them always seem a little crazier than people in strange-looking clothes sans weaponry. Whatever the popularity value, bullet belts are now a fashion regularity in the heavy-metal world. Motörhead and Venom made them popular, but Mayhem and Destruction made them infamous for being worn only by psychotic motherfuckers. So of course when I saw one dangling from a jewelry rack in St. Mark's Place, I knew it had to be mine.

▷

I thought it would be only fitting for me to wrap a string of ammo around the waist of my slacks. I snapped on my bullet belt, fitting it accordingly, and viewed myself in the mirror.

Yupocalypse Now. Perfect.

The phone rang thrice, with short, angry screams of electronic impatience. Shorter rings meant the doorbell, longer rings meant the phone — my folks had decided to replace our beautiful church-bell doorbell with one of those gross intercom numbers. I picked up the receiver and yelled for identification.

A faded, faraway voice said, "Um, hi, it's me."

The minute I opened the door to my room, I knew hell was about to break loose: Erica had guessed who had just arrived. The door to her room flung open, and she bounded down the stairs giddily. I leaped after her, taking them two at a time, listening to her squeal in laughter.

"Not gonna make it," she yelped. "I'm gonna meet her."

"Oh, yeah?"

"Yeah!"

"Oh, yeah?!"

"Yeeewhoop!" In a second, my sister was yanked off the stairs and thrown kicking and screaming over my shoulder, bitching about how uncool it was and how badly she was going to get me back. I placed her down in the living room and went to the door.

"Heeeello hello hello," I said, flinging the door open.

Sweet mother of God, but she was beautiful. I looked at her, standing there in a curvy little green dress and a pair of strapped-up heels. I wanted to kneel before her and kiss her hand and then throw her into my sports car so that we could drive attractively off into a Hollywood sunset.

However, I was a teenage metalhead, so instead I just said, "Wow. You look amazing. My parents want to meet you."

"Hello to you, too, darling," she said sexily, and then changed it with a "You're not actually wearing that belt, are you?"

"Yes. Yes, I am. My mom and dad want to meet you."

She rolled her eyes. "Anything to please my favorite Goth boy." (*PANG! I was not a fucking GOTH!!!*) "C'mon, show me off to the 'rents."

I brought her inside, shutting the door carefully behind us. I took her up a set of stairs and into the dining room, where my mother sat reading and my sister buzzed around her like a hummingbird. My dad glanced up from the paper, nodded, and went back to it.

"Mom, Dad, Erica, this is Melissa. Melissa, this is my mom, my dad, and my sister, Erica."

"Hi," Melissa said giddily, and waved her hand in a furious "hi" motion.

"Oh. My. God," gasped my sister. "Your shoes are so FAB!"

I could see both Melissa and my mother holding in giggles at my sister's brilliant commentary. She shook hands with both of them, giving a quick hello to my mother and the name of some sort of crappy, stupid, non-vintage store.

"Sam talks about you quite a lot," said my mother, smiling. "I'm glad I finally get to meet the face behind the legend."

"Oh, dear," my angel responded, blushing nervously, "there's a legend?" She was pulling the Charming Girlfriend Routine! I loved this girl!

My mother smiled warmly back and, giving me a glance, said, "You're going to take off that belt, right?"

"First impressions last forever."

Mom sighed. "That's what I'm afraid of. Be back by midnight, and drop Melissa off first."

We were out of the house in a couple of seconds, me pulling her almost forcefully out of my abode. We strolled down my block, a well-dressed, New York teen couple. I slowly became that which I never was and normally looked down upon, and strangely enough, I kind of enjoyed it. It dawned on me that maybe it was why Melissa had wanted me to take her to a show, because for one night, she could escape her world, her *scene*. Now it was my turn. Time for my metamorphosis.

"Do me a favor?" she asked, giving me an *I know you* glance.

"Anything."

"Give my friends a chance, okay? Don't just judge them by how they dress and the way they look or anything. They may seem preppy or whatever to you, but they're really good people."

I smiled and gave her a nod, adding, "Understood, dear."

We hopped a cab to some dark café/restaurant on the Upper East Side, the kind of place with a round table and a bunch of couches and overstuffed chairs where people in Oxford-style shirts drank coffee and smoked cigarettes even though it was against the law. The minute I saw the inside of Nitekap (quite a name, huh?), I felt out of place. My hands were too big, my legs didn't move properly, and my body bumped into anything even slightly in my way. Without the help of any narcotics or alcohol, I had become Conan.

Melissa's friends waved us over to an area in the corner where they were smoking cigarettes and sipping drinks that looked foreign and deliciously poisonous. She took my hand, as if I were some sort of small child, and tugged me playfully over to the gathering of her comrades.

When we reached them, she introduced us all. The four of them were:

Josh. Gelled hair. Spiked and bleached in the front. Dressed like a Wall Street executive in his off time. Wearing shades, which meant that, what with the current lighting, he was probably as blind as a bat. When he spoke, it sounded like he looked: "So, the infamous Sam. Finally." Gave the once-over: "Wow . . . nice belt."

Adrian. Twiggy Asian girl hanging off of Josh's arm. Too much dark makeup, and a purse way too tiny to carry it all. Greeted me with a smile and a wave. "You've got quite a reputation."

Kyle. Looked like the kind of kid I might like the most. Really tight vintage Led Zeppelin shirt and a pair of tight jeans. Converse high-tops. Red. Mussed-up brown hair. Shook my hand tightly. I was beginning to dig him before he spoke. "Dude, like, totally wicked cool to finally meet you, man, really." He looked me over and grinned. "Okay, your belt is, like . . . DUDE. Totally rockin', bro."

Leslie. Blond in a black tank top. A bit more meat on her than the rest of them. Gave me a big, toothy smile and, before I could say a word, stood up and gave me a hug. "It is SO COOL to meet you, Sam."

I grimaced as we sat. These people were fucking aliens to me. Silent, personal judgment flowed forth. I could tell they were waiting for me to say or do something so they could gauge me, so they could try and understand what "type" I was. I radiated awkwardness, fear, discomfort, and sweat. *Especially* sweat. I could feel the first droplets forming on my forehead and my back. This was going to be tricky.

Neutral first move: "Nice to meet you."

Melissa and I sat down on a huge, plush couch in the little circle of furniture and preps that we'd become part of. She yanked my arm around her shoulder and started chatting with her friends about something inane: movies, commercials, Vin

Diesel. The two guys were arguing about some girl, someone they'd both hooked up with, and discussing how angry it made them when she didn't swallow.

My skin crawled, my hair prickled, my spine curled. This place was choking me. I needed out.

Calm down, I thought. *Don't be the Fuck-Up. I'm sure they're fine.*

"Cuban, Sam?"

Snap, crackle, and pop: My inner monologue broke. I looked up to see a big brown phallic symbol being offered to me by Josh. Cigars. Thank God for my father. Now I had something to do/talk about/fiddle with.

"How Cuban are we talking about here?"

"Sorry?"

"Well, is this something that the guy at the Andy's Deli around your corner *told* you was a Cuban, or is it from Castro-loving Cuba?"

Josh smiled, very slow, very slightly, like I imagine the devil would when you take the pen from him and ask where the signature should go. "It's a real Cuban. My dad gets them from some of his connections. It's real good."

"Just so long as you're not handing me a piece of shit," I said smoothly.

"I'm sure it's better than whatever *you've* been smoking."

That smile. I wanted to peel it off and slap him with it. It was a rich boy's smile. A snob's sneer. I took his cigar and lit it with one of the candles resting on the table, puffing loudly and sending mushroom clouds of smoke up around my face.

"'S good," I said, flashing him my pearly whites.

"Lookit him," laughed Kyle, "total badass, man. Rock ON,

motherfucker." He reached out and gave me a little chuck on the shoulder. I faked a laugh and shrugged, to which he commented, "Oh, yeah, he fuckin' knows it! He's aaaaall about it! Yeah!"

The more Kyle talked, the more I wanted him to die cold and alone.

"Hey!" said Melissa, firing me a puerile glare. "No smoking!"

"But they're allowed to smoke!" I said, pointing at Josh and Kyle.

"Well, I'm not making out with them later," she pointed out. "But okay, tonight you can smoke." She gave me a big, full-mouthed grin, like a three-year-old who's proud of finishing all her vegetables. (PANG!!! *Any other day and you would rain fire and brimstone down on me for smoking! What the fuck is going on?*)

I held my own for a while, interjecting little bits of conversation, answering questions about myself, and trying to come across as charming and sophisticated. It didn't help that the more they talked, the more I hated these people, but I suppressed it. This night was important. One false move . . .

Melissa tugged my arm and turned me towards her. "Honey, tell Adrian that she's wrong."

I looked over at Adrian and said, "You're wrong."

Adrian shrugged. "I just think that the book was better than the movie, is all."

"What book? What movie?"

"*About a Boy.*"

"Oh," I said, and then turned to Melissa. "Then you're wrong."

She jabbed her tongue at me. "You're no fun." (*PANG: What the hell? You're smarter than this.*)

"Oh," said Adrian, puzzled, "you read?"

"Ex*cuse* me?!"

"Oh, no," she corrected, "I didn't mean, like, at all . . . I meant, for pleasure. Like, on your own."

"Oh. Yeah, of course."

She shrugged again. "You didn't sound like the type, I guess."

"I bet from what you heard, I sounded like the type to have twelve piercings, red eyeliner, tattoos all up and down my arms, a Coal Chamber shirt, black fingernails, maybe a dreadlock or two, a terrible drinking habit, and an empty brainpan? Lemme guess, I also worship the devil and like my steaks raw? Huh? Sound accurate?"

Adrian looked a little stunned, and managed to laugh out, "Whoa."

Stop it. Don't do this to yourself. Fuck that, don't do this to her.

"Sorry. Little high-strung. Meeting the friends and all."

"Right."

"What are you talking about? That CD sucks!" a voice shouted.

My ears perked up. Music? CD? What CD? Had somebody said something about music? Where? If I had a tail, it would have wagged. I turned to face Josh, who'd just announced that said CD sucked.

Music. I must be in the music conversation. This had to happen.

"Okay, dude, you have, like, totally no idea what you're saying." Kyle sighed. "That CD is probably one of the greatest rock records ever written. 'You Shook Me All Night Long'? Come on, dude. I mean, like . . . dude. Man."

Back in Black! They were having a conversation about AC/DC! Thank you, sweet mother of God!

"It's a primitive redneck rock album, Kyle."

"Now, that's just unfair," I said, pointing at Josh accusingly.

"How so?" he asked, treating me like an insect at his ear. Stories about Vlad the Impaler came to mind, though these had the word *Turk* replaced with *Josh*.

"You call *Back in Black* primitive," I said, scientific as all hell. "That's a lie, and it's unfair to say as such. That album alone proves that Angus Young is one of the greatest guitarists out there. There's so much *power* and so much *emotion* and so much . . . *umph* behind the guitars on that album —"

"Umph?!"

"— that it's, quite frankly, a dead-on *lie* to call it primitive. And while the majority of AC/DC fans are, granted, a little less classy than I'm sure you're used to, one can't help but admit that AC/DC's music, especially that on *Back in Black*, is extremely creative *and* technical, with loads of talent behind it —"

"Did you say 'umph'?"

"— while at the same time being brilliantly catchy. Seeing as the majority of music, especially hard rock and roll, is either one or the other but not usually *both*, that makes *Back in Black* one of the best rock records out there. Therefore, your claim is unfounded."

Until then, I guess it had just slipped my mind to observe the group. I was basically taken by the heavy-metal muse, as it were, and my love for the album containing "What Do You Do for Money, Honey?" had usurped all other parts of my brain. So I was pleasantly surprised when I finished my little commentary and discovered that our entire circle had gone mute and bug-eyed, staring at me.

And then they exploded.

"Dude!" howled Kyle, wide-eyed. "Dude, that was the shee-YIT right there, bro!" He slapped me five, rocking his head up and down in mock headbanging.

"Whoa again," said Adrian.

"A little obsessed, aren't we, Sam?" scoffed Josh with an eyebrow raised, smirking.

"There he goes," Melissa said, rubbing my head like I was a dog. "That's my little heavy-metal boyfriend again." (*PANG: I could not believe this. "There's my heavy-metal boyfriend?" Whatever happened to "You are not some fucking character, okay?"*)

"Oh, I dunno," giggled Leslie, "I thought it was kinda cool! He was so into it and —"

"Fatty!" snapped Josh. "Shush!" Leslie squealed in mock anger and shock, giving Josh a playful push and then looking away. I followed her eyes down to her drink, watched her sigh heavily, and read the feelings in her face. (*PANG: How could he SAY something like that?! Why didn't she fight back? Why isn't she going nuts?!*)

Turning back to me, Josh said, "You might want to see somebody for that, boy." (*PANG: Why wasn't I going nuts?!*)

"Oh, God," Melissa chuckled, "you should hear him alone! Metal this, metal that, it just goes on and on . . ."

PANG.

PANG.

PANG PANG PANG.

PANGPANGPANGPANGPANGPANGPA —

snap

"Why are you doing this?" I asked through clenched teeth.

Again, silence took over.

"Wh . . . what?" she laughed.

"Why are you treating me like . . . like your damn trophy husband? Or . . . or, like your pet?"

She smiled confusedly. "What are you talk —"

"I mean, this entire time, you've been showing me off like some sort of prize fucking poodle with spikes, while your damn Upper East Side friends sit around in this circle of fucking idiocy and judgment, and you just go along with it. Whatever happened to Shakespeare, or mythology, or any of the other things you love? Do you ALWAYS become this when you're around them?"

Her smile was gone. She stared at me with what looked like horror, her face reading clear as day: *Don't do this right now.*

Part of me screamed the same thing. *She's right. Don't be the Fuck-Up.* Another part of me roared back at it. This felt good. This felt right. I needed this.

"Christ, kid," spat Josh, "calm the fuck down!"

"YOU!" I said, whipping around to face him, pointing at him in utter contempt. "You are a sad fucking excuse for a human being! You've been talking to me as if you're my father this entire time, with a smirk on your face and your smug, domineering attitude. You're lucky we're in a public establishment, 'boy.'" I leaned in close. "Because, otherwise, the minute you called that poor girl 'fatty,' I would've smacked you around like a redheaded stepchild."

"*Someone's* a bit of a psycho . . ."

"I'd rather be a psycho than a DKNY elitist worm like you, Josh."

"Sam, maybe you should —" Melissa began.

"And you! Leslie!" I whipped around, light in my eyes. I was on a roll. "There's no way you can actually *enjoy* being called a fatty! Next time he calls you that, I say bury one of those fucking uncomfortable-looking heels in his crotch!"

"Sam!"

"Adrian, you seem okay, just a little misinformed," I said. "Eat something, though. Christ."

"Hells, yeah, baby!" shouted Kyle. "Fuckin' rebellion, dude! That's what I'm all about, bro!"

"NO!" I snarled, turning to him. "I am not your bro, or your boy, or anything resembling your homey! Not at all! You have your heart in the right place, but, man, you need to learn how to fucking speak properly! You sound like a reject out of a bad *Clueless* parody. Jesus, all of you people make me want to fucking murder something!"

Silence for the third time. If they weren't staring at me in disgust before, they sure as hell were now. I looked around the circle we sat in, one by one taking in the horrified faces of the people I'd just chewed out, until . . .

. . . until I got to her. She sat right beside me, her arm squeezing the life out of my shoulder, with a face molded out of sheer disbelief. Her eyes vacant, her mouth hanging open like some sort of fish, with a question hanging from her entire face: *Why did you do this?*

Melissa. The best thing I had going for me in my life right now.

I had fucked up. Again.

"All right," I whispered, standing shakily, "I'm going to go now." I stepped over the couch I'd been sitting on and slowly made my way to the open door, to the cool open night air, away from the murky lighting and the too-soft couches. I felt like I was having an out-of-body experience. I could honestly not believe what I'd done.

I got out on the sidewalk and waved my arm desperately to hail a cab. I needed to get home. I needed to get home and cry and listen to metal and not be anywhere near here anymore. The last thing I ever needed was something like her following me out of the restaurant and onto the sidewalk.

But she did. Of course.

chapter 18
Practice What You Preach

▷

"What the fuck was that, Sammy Markus?"

I decided to try it again.

"Run away with me."

"What?"

"Run away with me. Come on. I can get some money. We can just leave."

"Leave what? What are you talking about?"

"LEAVE! Leave this! Leave New York and everyone we know!"

"What did you think you were doing back there?"

"You don't *need* those people, Melissa. You don't need the —"

"I don't need these people, Sammy? I *like* these people! These are my *friends*, not a bunch of drunken losers!"

"What?"

"You heard me! So *what* if I'm different with them than I am with you? You're my *boyfriend*, Sammy! That's the point! You do that, too!"

"Not *that* different. Never. You've never been like that. That's . . . that's . . ."

Her words from after the Deicide show dawned on me.

"That's the side of you *I've* never seen, isn't it?"

"Christ, why are you doing this tonight?"

"Well, because I'm tired of you and your idiot twit friends treating me like a goddamn child, how about that? I'm tired of you becoming what you became. It didn't take me too long to figure out that one."

"What does that mean?"

"It means . . . it means you were so fucking *different* back there, with those people, than you are with me that it makes me angry . . ."

"I should've known. I should have known you'd pull something like this."

"What? What do you mean by that?"

"I mean YOU, with your childishness and your selfish fucking attitude! You just can't accept other people!"

"What?!"

"You're so . . . *unique*, but you're so damn close-minded!"

"I'm dating *you*."

"No. Y'know what? No. This is not about me. This is about you. This is about what you just did."

"I spoke my mind!"

"You embarrassed me in front of a bunch of my closest friends!"

"What does it matter what they think of me?"

"What does — it matters because *you're my boyfriend*. Because I brought you here to meet them. I didn't expect you to go fucking nuts!"

"I spoke my mind —"

"Yeah, yeah, you spoke your mind, and y'know what? It's a pretty sick place in there."

". . . So this is how you feel about me?"

"After what just happened, I don't *know* how I feel about you, Sammy."

"I just . . . I just . . ."

"You just *what?*"

A moment of thought. Then:

"Y'know what really matters in my life right now?"

"What, Sammy?"

"Heavy metal and you. That's it."

"What?"

"That's it. That's all that matters right now. Heavy metal music and you. All I really have in the world are my CDs and you. All I care about, all I give a shit about. Heavy metal and you. And now I'm going to lose half of everything that matters to me because my thoughts just slipped out for a second."

"Oh, right. Like a three-minute rant just slips out here and there."

"I'm serious."

"So am I. Good night, Sam."

"Where are you going?"

"Back inside."

"Back to *them?!*"

"*Them?!* Yes, back to them. *They* are my friends, Sam!"

"I love you."

145

"No. No. Don't do this."

"I love you. I'm sorry. I love you."

"Oh, God, Sammy . . ."

"Please."

She stood firmly. She scrunched her face.

"Good night, Sam."

And she went back to them.

chapter 19
Wait and Bleed

And then I woke up.

"Good morning, Sam!"

Erica had poked her head into my room, grinning stupidly. I glared groggily at her.

"What do you want?"

"Scotch tape?"

"Mph. Over on the side of my desk with all the paper scraps. Look under that issue of *Metal Maniacs*."

She walked over and inspected my desk. "You mean *Terrorizer*?"

"Ungh. 'S got hairy Swedish men in facepaint on it?"

"Looks that way."

"That's it."

My sister grabbed the Scotch tape. Instead of leaving, though, she sat down at my desk and faced me, smiling giddily.

I gave her the most evil eye I could muster and growled, "What time is it?"

"Around ten-thirty."

"Why are you still here?"

"Be*cause*," she sang, "I want to hear all about your date with Melissa!"

I could actually feel the stare come out of my body, and apparently she could, too. Erica's face fell to a look of peril, as if she were about to run a marathon through a minefield.

"That bad, huh?"

"Let's just say," I grumbled, slamming my face back down into the pillow, "that it could have gone much, much better."

"Ooooh. I'm sorry."

"Don't pity me," I mumbled.

My sister fell silent. She finally began to leave, but right before she walked out she said, "Don't lose your marbles, Sam. Don't let her get to you."

I heard the door slam before I mumbled "fuck you" into the pillow.

Since it was Sunday, and since the night before had been such a God-awful disaster, I decided not to get up until about eleven. Instead, I spent a good deal of time lying facedown on my bed, cursing myself out. I just couldn't understand it. Why? Why in hell would you *ever* do something like that, Sammy Markus? Hadn't the realization been that it would be better to adapt and save this relationship than stand firm and ruin it? Wasn't this too perfect to lose due to lack of flexibility, you ass?

I rolled onto my back and studied the ceiling. Maybe there couldn't be any adaptation. I'd been trying my best, feeling myself adapt in little ways that were big deals to me. But perhaps I was kidding myself. Maybe this whole thing was doomed from the start, cursed to burn out in an explosion of tears and enraged phone conversations. What a pleasant thought.

I wanted to die. Actually, it wasn't that: I wanted to be alone. Alone with her. I wanted to go back, back before last night, and obliterate everyone on Earth but me and her. I wanted to have been able to wake up this Sunday morning with her, warm and soft, cupped in my arms. And it wasn't like that. Because I'd fucked up.

Marilyn Manson. This was a Manson moment. I threw *Holy Wood* into my stereo and basked in the sheer misanthropic bliss of it all. Mother's milk for unrequited love and intense self-loathing.

At eleven, I yanked my body out of bed and threw on a T-shirt and pants, deciding that I might as well be hard on myself with a full stomach. I slumped down the stairs and into our kitchen, following the smell of eggs and toast. I found my mother and father at the kitchen table, reading the newspaper and sipping coffee.

"Hey, honey!" my mom cooed.

"You shouldn't listen to your music that loud," my dad said. "It'll hurt your ears."

"You mean it hurts *your* ears."

My dad looked up. "What? What do you mean?"

I shrugged. "If you want me to turn down my music because it annoys you, just say so. Don't give me some sort of ear health thing."

He frowned. "You okay?"

"Nope."

"You wanna talk about it?"

"Nope."

"Fair enough." He went back to his paper. My parents knew that my *no*s were not *please talk to me*s in disguise. When I said I didn't want to talk, I didn't want to talk.

As I poured myself a cup of coffee (black, three scoops of sugar) and scraped together what was left of a pan of scrambled eggs (salt and ketchup), my mom walked up behind me and put a hand on my shoulder (obviously concerned).

"Melissa?"

"Mmm-hrm."

"You two not you two anymore?"

"I really don't know."

I felt the hand give me a little squeeze. "Just do what feels right," she said honestly.

"Thanks." I meant it. One thing I appreciated about my parents was that they didn't consider my love life to be just another series of "teenage romances." They didn't blow my relationships off like most parents did. They took me seriously.

"Welcome." And then, almost as an afterthought, "Don't put too much sugar in your coffee."

I sighed and walked back up to my room, sipping as I went.

The day got progressively grayer. I tried to call her twice, but both times her mother told me that she was out (I could almost see frost coating the mouthpiece, the woman was so cold). I decided immediately after breakfast that I would visit her at her apartment tonight, just to talk, to see if I could salvage whatever was left of this thing that had changed my life in the past two months. To bow my head and let her know I was wrong.

I was dying for a cigarette, but at the same time the idea was somewhat repulsive. I wanted to go out, but when I grabbed my boots and began to lace them, all desire to leave the house simply flew from my mind. The thought of calling Irish or Brent to get some bitching and moaning done crossed my mind, but I quickly dismissed it — I could almost hear the *I told you sos* and the *doesn't deserve yous*. Besides, they had seemed so distant recently. Every time we talked, there was the general feeling that lots of things were going unsaid, and my current comfort level was so low that the idea of anything even slightly awkward was utterly loathsome to me.

I was in emotional limbo. Which meant only one thing.

I sat down and did my homework.

It all felt strangely appropriate — doing my homework was so mechanical, so formal. Math: rewrite the problem in my notebook, write out each step for the problem, underline the answer when done. Chemistry: read the question, go back to the chapter I was supposed to have read and look for that answer, type the final solution. History was pretty much the same as chemistry, and all I had to do for English was finish Dostoyevsky. Homework finally had some place in my life: the thing to do when the rest of my heart and my head weren't ready for the world.

As I put down *Crime and Punishment*, I heard my mother yell, "Sam! Phone!" I walked over to my cordless and picked it up.

"Yeah?"

"So what are you going to do about this girl, bucko?"

Carver. The coolest, nicest, dumbest, craziest, most admirable, most angering human being in my life. He's not heavy (or metal, for that matter). He's my brother.

"First things first — I'm going to beat you with a bike chain for continuing to call me that, *bucko*. How's Brown?"

"'S nice. Nice people. Good classes. Tell me about this girl."

"How'd you know about her?"

"Mom just told me about you being all hating-in-the-dark this morning. Talk to me." I could almost hear him smiling through the phone. "Bucko."

"Do you really care?" I sighed.

"That's the dumbest question I've ever heard," he barked. "Spill it."

So I spilled it. Everything from when me and Melissa met to last night, when I finally let my *pangs* come flying out of my mouth like romantic shrapnel. I told him about the way she made me feel that spectacular feeling, like it was just me and her in the world, and like I was the light of her life, and about how she angered me sometimes, about how I couldn't believe someone this wonderful could be this cruel. I told him about her living room, about how special she thinks I am, and about the sidewalk, about how crazy she thought I was. I told him about the character she didn't believe me to be, but the one she'd finally accepted me as. He powdered the conversation with *uh-huh*s and *okay, right*s, until I finally came to a halt and said, "And that's about the whole story."

There was a pause. Carver whistled, then said, "Looks like you're in quite a spot here, Sam."

"Oh, thanks for the notice, asshole."

"Look. Think about your life for the past . . . how long has this been going on?"

I shrugged, even though he couldn't see it. "I dunno. Two months."

"Wow! You've really dedicated yourself to this girl in two months, bucko."

"Stop calling me that."

"No. Anyway . . . well, you seem devoted to her. You seem like you really care about her. The question is: Do you think she's the right person for you?"

"I just fucking *told* you, man. She's incredible. She's perfect. She's everything —"

"Sam. Shut up. That's baby talk. Think about your relationship with her. Think about you two as a couple. Think good and hard. What do you feel like?"

I thought. I thought good and hard. About the concert, and the night out with her friends, and about that night alone in front of the movie, and about the promises I made to her. I thought about my life since I met her. Good and hard. And the thing that came to me most was surprising.

"I feel," I said, reluctant to admit that he was right, "like I've been trying to be good enough for her."

"Solid. And are you?"

I shrugged again. "Apparently not."

"Do you think you're going to be any time soon?"

"No?"

"Is that a question?"

"No."

"Right. Now here's the deal, Sammy." Carver inhaled, signaling that he was about to impart a great deal of wisdom upon me. I braced myself.

"I admire you. I've always admired you. I've admired you because you've always known you. You've always known yourself, always been yourself, and have never compromised who you want to be. Even when I've thought you were being a dick, or acting stupid, or a hopeless geek, you'd be who you wanted to be. Me, being myself, took me some time to figure out. But you, with your scary movies and your heavy metal and all that shit . . . you just acted like yourself. And that, bucko, is why I always admired you."

If my tongue hadn't frozen like a slab of meat in a locker, I would've said something. But I didn't. I just sat there in silence. Carver waited a bit, then continued.

"Now from what you're saying, this girl is pretty great. And you care about her a lot. But you need to talk to her about you. About how you feel, and the way you are, and how she can't make you change that. You can't feel like you're not good enough forever, kid. Don't, y'know, be a dick to her or anything, 'cause from the way you talk about it, you really adore her. But don't let her change you. That's not who you are."

I struggled for words through my corpse of a tongue, but all I could get out was, "Um. Wow."

"Yeah, well, that's my opinion."

"Um. Thanks. Thanks a lot. I'll, um, see what I can do."

"Good to hear it, Sam. Do me a favor?"

"Sure."

"Keep this conversation just between us."

"Right."

"Later, bucko."

And the phone clicked off in my ear, leaving me to that eerie silence disconnected conversations have. That was so like Carver, to give the last word and bolt, pretending he never uttered a word.

I glanced at the clock. It was 5:49. I'd spent too long here. I'd gotten all my homework done. It was a Sunday night; technically, with my work finished, I was allowed to leave my house.

I grabbed my coat and rushed to the door. Time to make amends.

chapter 20
Terrible Certainty

▷

As I started walking down her street, I realized that I had no idea what I was going to say.

The first things that ran into my mind were apologies, end-less demands for forgiveness and warmth. But then Carver's words hit me, and I wasn't so sure I really wanted to apologize. Maybe I'd just gush, let the words and feelings flow out, and see what happened. But then again, didn't gushing get me into this whole mess in the first place? There had to be some sort of planned, intelligent way to let her know how I truly —

Josh's jacket came into my view. Right next to hers.

I stopped dead in my tracks, a squealing-brake sound going through my mind. There they were. Walking towards her house together. Just talking. Friends. I slowed, calmed, told my heart to stop beating like the bass drum in a Carcass song. I slowly shifted to my left, hoping and praying they wouldn't accidentally see me. My watcher's instinct kicked in. They had no idea I was there.

They stopped and turned towards each other, both of them in profile to me. I tried reading lips, but it was no use; I could only make out what they meant by body language.

Melissa: smiled lightly, gave a little shake of the head. *Thank you.*

Josh: shook head while looking at the ground. *No problem.* Looked back up at her and threw out his thumb, hitchhiker style. *Anyway, I should be going.*

Melissa: smiled, extended arms for a hug. *Bye.*

Josh: gave Melissa a big strong hug. *Bye.*

Melissa: pulled out of the hug, kept arms around Josh's shoulders, stared Josh straight in the eyes.

Josh: kept arms on her sides, kept staring into her eyes.

Melissa: glanced timidly at her feet, looked back into his eyes.

Josh: reached up a hand and brushed her hair out of her face.

Melissa: gave a short chuckle.

Something in my stomach crawled. I imagined it was a dead emotion. A near-dead one, anyway.

Pang.

Josh: tapped Melissa on the lips with his index finger, smiled contentedly, and strolled away.

Melissa: stared long after Josh, took a deep breath, walked back inside.

Sam: turned and bolted.

⬜⬜

She was never like that with me.

She was never that comfortable with me. She could never hold me like that, without *meaning* anything, without it being about sex or comforting me after a crying fit or something like that. There was always the feeling of relationship politics with us, with one of us worried about how the other would feel about this or that. Even when she made me feel wonderful, it was always something I acknowledged — *she just did something really sweet. That's so great.* And there she was, holding him like I would hold a friend like Ivy, with nothing sexual or awkward about it.

And I couldn't stop them. I couldn't even speak to her. Because after one look at the two of them, it was obvious that she had something with him that was naturally right. Something that worked like it should. And knowing who he was, and knowing she could feel like that for him, I realized that everything I'd felt was bullshit.

All the effort and worry we'd put into this relationship was worthless. Because she could never feel like that for me.

▷

My feet refused to carry me any farther than that. I wanted, desperately, to slug him, to tear his guts out, to watch her soul get wrenched to pieces by hooks of ice. But all I could do was walk. Walk away. Keep my head down. And walk away from her and him and that fingertip on her lips. Burned into my mind with a branding iron. The spiral of his fingertip on her soft lips. My hell.

I got home quickly enough: There was no stroll to my walk, none of the normal casualness I put into it. It was mechanical. I just walked. I slammed the door behind me and went upstairs to my room, not bothering to even try to talk to my parents or my sister. It would only hurt them. I would only bathe them in my hate. I'd hurt enough people so far. The only one left was myself.

The minute I walked through my door, it came into my head.

Slayer.

Second page, first disc. *Seasons in the Abyss.* I slammed it in, stood in front of the speakers, and let it hit.

"War Ensemble" kicked in. I felt the music, the power, the hate and the love and the hurt, all coursing through my body, my veins, my nerves, and on up to my eyes. I cried. I cried hard. Not hard like sobbing and blubbering, hard like a rock. My face was a ball of tightened muscles with two burning razor-rivers flowing down the sides of it.

"PROPAGANDA DEATH ENSEMBLE, BURIAL TO BE! CORPSES ROTTING THROUGH THE NIGHT IN BLOOD-LACED MISERY! SCORCHED EARTH: THE POLICY, THE REASON FOR THE SIEGE!"

We were nothing. I was the Fuck-Up.

I came alive.

Whirling, I felt my entire body tighten, twist, pull. My fingers clenched. My arms bulged. I couldn't feel anything but *it*. The granddaddy of all pangs.

The window.

"THE PENDULUM IT SHAVES THE BLADE; THE STRAFING AIR BLOOD RAID!"

I rushed it, my fist up like a scorpion's tail. Everything around me blurred in a rush of speed and anger, the window my sole focus.

"INFILTRATION, PUSH RESERVES, ENCIRCLE THE FRONT LINE! SUPREME ART OF STRATEGY PLAYING ON THE MINDS!"

All the effort and the stupidity for nothing. I fucked up. This was me. The window.

"BOMBARD 'TIL SUBMISSION! TAKE ALL TO THEIR GRAVES! INFILTRATION OF TRIUMPH — THE NUMBERS THAT ARE DEAD!"

Wham — my fist slammed into the glass of the window with all of the strength I could muster. A cry, of pain and rage, escaped my mouth. A lightning-bolt crack split the windowpane.

This seemed familiar. Vaguely.

"SPORT THE WAR!"

I raised my fist again.

"WAR SUPPORT!"

Wham — a second collision. My fingers screamed in pain. A second crack, stemming from the first, wrenched through the glass. It reminded me of my heart.

"THE SPORT IS WAR, TOTAL WAR! WHEN VICTORY IS A MASSACRE!"

And something else. This was so familiar. Where? Where was I remembering this?

"THE FINAL SWING IS NOT A DRILL —"

I raised my fist again. Salinger.

"IT'S HOW MANY PEOPLE I CAN KILL!"

I froze. J. D. Salinger, *Catcher in the Rye*. Holden Caulfield breaks all of the windows in his house. When his brother dies. The one with the poetry-covered baseball mitt.

I was just repeating something from a teenage drama. That was my life: a stereotype. Heartbroken adolescent misfit. I couldn't believe it. Christ, even my grief was unoriginal.

I rushed to my stereo and pushed the EJECT button, grabbing my Slayer CD and throwing it into my Discman. I couldn't be here any longer. I needed to leave, to walk, to escape. There were too many reminders. A Shakespeare paperback, or a Deicide CD, or the glaring cracks in the window, staring me down.

I ran down the stairs, trying not to get noticed by my family, pumping Slayer, sweet Slayer, into my eardrums. As I passed the den, I could just make out my mother calling my name —

"Sam?"

— before I rushed past her and bolted down the stairs. Out the front door. Up the block as quickly as I possibly could.

It dawned on me, just as I started walking downtown, that I hadn't taken my coat off when I got home.

chapter 21
Nemesis Divina

▷

Before I knew it, Times Square had risen up around me. It was surprisingly happening for a Sunday night. I looked up and was greeted by bright lights, theater ads, the Virgin Megastore, and a giant Cup O' Noodles. I hadn't noticed how fast I was walking until then — I'd just been letting my feet carry me, and Slayer control me. Rage or hate or whatever horrible black burning thing I was feeling rushed through my system, tearing me to pieces. And y'know what? I think it showed.

People started avoiding me. The crowd parted as I walked through it. Couples would disconnect their hands and let me walk between them. Flocks of squealing girls would split open and let me through. Tough guys, rough unshaven old dudes who normally gave me a hard time, looked at me with high eyebrows and stepped aside. And it felt *good*, dammit. Like having a protective bubble of fire surrounding me, my broken heart embodied. I wanted everyone to know my pain and my rage, to understand that no one would ever hurt me like that again. My spikes went from jewelry to armor, my coat became a cloak of black feelings.

Anthrax lyrics popped into my head, the words to a song called "In My World." *I am not afraid, I am not afraid, nothing touches me — I'm a walking razor blade.*

Amen to that.

A woman didn't see me coming, and then it was too late, her shoulder colliding with mine. I looked her in the eyes and snarled, "Watch where you're going, you stupid bitch." Her face changed; she looked like she was about to cry. I hoped she would.

You see, Melissa? I thought. *Y'know that side you told me you never wanted to see again? Well, you just brought it out, honey. You and that preppy bastard. I'm going to let it reign. This is your fault. You did this to me.*

The 40-numbered streets turned into the 30s, and then the 20s, and then the Teens, and when I finally stopped, I was at St. Marks, right in front of the Cube. The Cube is brilliant — a massive sculpture of a cube balancing on one of its corners, known as a hangout for Goths and punks. I trudged over to it, ignoring traffic, and, upon reaching it, took a seat on the little concrete platform it rested on.

This was it. This was what I'd become.

I felt myself collapse.

My face crumpled, my back curled, and I fell into a little fetal ball, clumped up at the base of the Cube without a person in sight, angry Californian thrash metal streaming into my ears. I bawled and blubbered and caked my palms in snot and tears and spit. I took deep breaths to try and calm myself down, and instead just heaved massive sobs into my hands. No one to save me. No one to care. Just depression, Slayer, and me.

I sat, balled up and weeping into my knees, for I don't know how long. Eventually, the CD spun down to the last song, and as Tom Araya belted out the refrain of "Seasons in the Abyss," I managed to stop my sobs and calm my ragged breathing. The last guitar riff faded out, and my Discman gave its dying beep. I felt alone.

A hand came down softly on my shoulder, and a voice whispered, "Sam?"

I looked over my shoulder and into Ivy's face. I hadn't seen her in ages — we'd had coffee maybe three months ago — and she'd changed thoroughly since then. She was still her usual adorably curvy self, but her style had gone bonkers. Her plaid pants were now a leather handcuffed skirt, her T-shirt had become a stitched-up amalgam of fabrics, like Sally in *The Nightmare Before Christmas*. Her red Converse All-Stars were cherry-colored Doc Martens with polka dots, and her bright-green hair had changed to white with black roots. Out of her lip stuck a single metal spike.

I sniffed. "Hi, Ivy."

"Hi, Sam," she said softly. "You okay?"

"Nah," I said, shaking my head.

"Wanna talk about it?"

I nodded.

She turned to her side, and I saw Pyro standing behind her. Pyro was a squatter down on St. Marks who worked as a DJ in his spare time — a really cool, really amiable guy. We'd never gotten to know each other well enough.

"Hey, I'll see you later, okay?" she cooed to him. He nodded knowingly and walked off towards Union Square. Ivy plopped down beside me and pulled a cigarette from behind her ear, popping it into her mouth and lighting it in a single, swift motion. She offered me one. I was about to turn her down, but then thought, *Why not? No one's stopping me.* I took a smoke and borrowed her light.

"So, how've you been, man?" she said, patting me lightly on the back. "Haven't seen you in a while. Dan mentioned he saw you at the Deicide show."

"I've been . . . around. Doing okay, I guess." Gag. Why had I never realized how *bad* these things tasted?!

"You," she said, mockingly accusatory, "have been sucked in by this rich uptown private school bullshit, that's what! Fiend!"

I scoffed. "You go to an uptown private school, too!"

"Not ze point!" she barked in a German accent. "So . . . what's going on? Why are you so glum?"

I sighed. "Girl stuff."

"Ah," she said. "Wanna tell me about it?"

I shrugged. "Got nothing better to do."

So I told her. Everything. She nodded, and smiled occasionally, and stared pensively out into space while smoking. And when I got to the part about seeing Melissa with Josh and running down here, she put up her hand to signal that she'd heard enough.

"Two months, you say?"

"Maybe a little more."

"Sammy Markus. Always rushing into love."

"Hey, now, not always —"

"You rushed in with me."

I said nothing.

"So," she said, "are you going to stay with her?"

"Would you?"

"It doesn't matter what *I would* do, Sammy. What matters is what *you will do*." She stared off into space some more, and then abruptly rose to her feet. "Get up."

"Why?" I asked, puzzled.

"Because."

"Because why?"

"Because we're playing RAMP. Now, get up."

RAMP. Jesus, I'd totally forgotten. We'd made it up so long ago. Leave it to Ivy to remember Romantic Advice Marco Polo.

I stood up, brushing off my pants. "I'm It, I suppose?"

"You're the one who needs advice. You remember all of the rules?"

I closed my eyes, darkness surrounding me. "As if I could ever forget."

"Okay . . . ready . . . set . . . go!"

My hands shot out in front of me like a bad Boris Karloff parody. "Do you think I should go back to her? Marco."

"Polo. Tough to say. *I* wouldn't, personally. After realizing just how . . . *off* you two are in your relationship, do you really want to go back to her?" Forward and to my left. I stumbled towards the sound, and heard footsteps twirl around me.

"I don't know, I mean . . . I still really care about her a lot. Marco."

"Polo. Well, I understand, but really, Sammy, caring about someone doesn't mean you two would be perfect together." Right behind me. I wheeled on my feet and stumbled forward. She giggled.

"That's the thing: I feel like I caused this, like maybe we could have worked if I had just kept myself under control. Marco."

"Polo. While I admit you could've been more tactful with expressing your thoughts, hon," she said, a little to my right and forward, "you basically just vented what she was making you feel. It doesn't make you a bad person to feel that way." I lunged forward, swinging my arm out. My fingers slapped against the smooth side of the Cube.

"True. But, I mean . . . maybe I should hear her side of the story. Marco."

"Polo. So go talk to her. Tell her how you feel. See what she says." Forward. I shambled out, my arms swinging wildly.

"You think we should give it another try?"

No response.

"Ivy? You think I should —"

It hit me.

"Marco."

"Polo. Took you long enough. *That* I'm not so sure about. You should see what she has to say, fir —" But before she could finish, I leaped to my left and grabbed her wrist, laughing happily as I won.

Ivy sighed. "You got me. I can't believe it. You haven't gotten me in a while."

"You talked too much this time." A pause. "So you think I should see her and try to talk it over?"

She shrugged. "Yeah. That's my opinion, anyway. Take some time and work out all of the knots. Don't be too hard on her, but think about yourself. Think about what you need, okay?"

"I will," I said softly. "Thanks, Ivy. Thanks so much."

She smiled. "Just helping a boy who used to treat me well. Gimme a hug, you moron."

I walked over to her and clutched her in my arms, trying to squeeze enough of her into myself so that I could store it in me.

"You look tired," she whispered in my ear. "Take a cab home tonight, okay?"

I took her up on that advice, blowing the last of my money on taxi fare. By the time I got home, between the crying and the walking and the RAMP, I was too tired to even try and deal with my parents or my work or any such thing. I undressed and crawled into bed, falling asleep the minute my head touched the pillow.

chapter 22
Before Dishonor

I can't really describe it perfectly enough, so I'll put it in lay-man's terms: The next morning *sucked.*

I crawled out of bed with the sound of Soilwork blasting from my stereo, just conscious enough to remember Melissa and Josh outside of her building. I prayed a quick shower would change my sentiment, but alas, it didn't help in the least. I stood in the spray, not really feeling the water, wishing that the world would just open up and swallow me *and* my shower.

Finally, after putting on my clothes, I sent Melissa an e-mail reading:

M —

Expect me at your place today. 4:15. We have a lot to talk about, I know. Let's see if we can work this out, okay?

I miss you. See you then.
— *Sammy*

It was Monday. What was first period Monday? Gym? Yup, physical education with Coach Skinner, a towering wrinkled man who loved calling me a sniveler when I asked to be let into the weight room early. There was no way I was going to that class right now. Instead, I opened my burning program, raided my CaseLogic, and went to work on her new mix:

1. Nine Inch Nails, "Something I Can Never Have"
2. GWAR, "I Hate Love Songs"
3. Pantera, "This Love"
4. Pat Benatar, "Love Is a Battlefield"
5. Slipknot, "Everything Ends"
6. Green Day, "F.O.D."
7. Corporation 187, "Violated Relation"
8. Stabbing Westward, "Torn Apart"
9. Darkane, "Submission"
10. The Misfits, "Die, Die, My Darling"
11. Marilyn Manson, "The Last Day on Earth"
12. Anthrax, "Only"
13. Metallica, "The Unforgiven"
14. Slayer, "213"
15. The Smashing Pumpkins, "Zero"

I adorned the cover with a drawing of a crying man running off of a cliff, not able to see his way because his face is buried in his hands.

I wrote *The Fool* at the top in curling script.

Done. Music that spoke. I hoped she'd listen.

As I finished my cereal and threw my backpack onto my shoulders, my mother came downstairs and stopped me.

"What happened to your window last night?"

The number of excuses I could come up with was uncannily large. However, they all made me feel like a rat. Last night had been important enough to me that I didn't feel like lying about any of it to anybody.

"I punched the shit out of it."

Her eyes widened and darted to my fists. "Oh my God! Are you okay?"

Warmth rushed through me. That was the reaction I hadn't been expecting, but wanted desperately. "Yeah, I'm fine. Sorry about that. I just had to vent some steam."

"Well," she sighed, "it's not great, but it's just a window. We'll see what we can do about fixing those cracks." As she walked back up the stairs, she glanced over her shoulder and smirked. "Holden."

Damn, she was good.

I trudged off to school with the sense of edge I had from the night before still brilliantly intact. It wasn't that I hated everyone, I just used my appearance to try and ward people off. I didn't want to be stared at or thought about or noticed in the least. My scowl was as pronounced as I could make it; I bared my spikes like quills. I wanted a sign on my forehead for everyone to see: PLEASE, FOR YOUR OWN SAKE, LEAVE ME BE.

As I stomped into my school's front hallway, Brent and Irish were just on their way out for a morning smoke. They waved at me and yelled something in my direction.

"What?" I said, holding my ear out.

"I said," said Irish, "that you can thank your mom for me."

I played along, cynically. "And why's that?"

"She'll know, my friend." He smirked. "She'll know."

"You're a real fuckin' riot, Irish. I swear. I'm dying."

They caught the vibe immediately, their faces changing from stupidly amused to suddenly concerned. "Christ," Irish said, and eyebrow raised, "what's in your ass today?"

I cleared the issue with one sentence: "I think I might end up breaking up with Melissa today."

They were at my sides in seconds, their eyes wide and their hands on my shoulders. "Shit, man, I'm sorry," whispered Irish. "I didn't, I mean, dude, I really —"

"It's fine, dude. You didn't know. It's fine."

"What's up?" said Brent eagerly. "She cheat on you?"

"No. I just . . . figured some things out last night."

"She's cheating on you, isn't she?"

"I told you, no. That's not the point."

"You know, you could tell us. If she was."

"Okay, leave it, Brent."

". . . Do we know the guy?"

"LEAVE IT, BRENT," I snarled.

"Dude, I just —"

"You just what?" I challenged. "She didn't cheat on me! There are no juicy details to relate! I just fucking figured out that no matter how much I love her, I'm not sure I can be with her. Christ, I come to school hoping you'll help me forget all this, and instead you just slam me in the face with it! Just! Fucking! Drop it!"

Brent's face screwed up, and he glanced to the side. He had his shades on, so I couldn't see his eyes, but I could tell that he wasn't happy. Brent's like that with feelings — when they're put right in front of his face, he goes from debonair to fidgety and uncomfortable in a few seconds. I realized that this wasn't helping my case, so I sighed and tried to explain my outburst.

"Look, man, it's just —"

"Nah," he said softly. "Nah, it's fine."

"Can I join you guys for a smoke?"

"Sure," he said in a trying-to-sound-like-his-normal-self voice. "Let's roll."

We went out to our stoop and smoked in silence. I spent most of the time just wondering why I'd smoked in the first place: The things tasted so fucking *gross* now. Irish looked plain stumped, as if he really didn't know what to say or do. Brent shook his head occasionally, or gave one of his customary little chuckles, but didn't say anything. But then again, one thing about Brent we all knew was that he hated a break in the conversation. He hated feeling awkward. So he finally started talking.

"Well," he said, "'tis better to have loved and lost and whatnot."

"Yeah, try it," I snapped a little too loudly.

"Geez, dude," he muttered.

"Don't 'geez, dude' me, Brent. I mean it. Once *you've* had your heart ripped out instead of just hooking up and ducking out, you can call me."

"Hey, wow, look, Sam," he said as calm as he could. "It's just, wow, that's mean. Don't be mean."

"Yeah, well, then quit being a fuck and start being my friend, how 'bout that?"

There was a silence, a nice little pause where I could almost feel the heat rising from Brent's body. I knew that he wanted to just open up on me, but that he wouldn't.

Well, I knew wrong.

The next thing I knew, Brent grabbed the nape of my neck and thrust me off of the stoop. I hit the curb with a lovely thud.

"You asshole!" I yelled, scrambling to my hands and knees. It was no use — by the time I got on one knee, Brent had descended the stoop and sent the sole of his foot slamming into my sternum. I fell on my back, sprawled out onto the concrete, tangled up in my overcoat and desperately trying to get my bearings. Was this really happening? Was Brent, Brent my good friend, actually beating the piss out of me?

My question was answered quickly as a hand snagged the collar of my shirt, yanking me into a sitting position. I got one quick glance of Brent's scrunched-up face, his eyes full of anger . . . and hurt? Was that hurt in his eyes? It didn't matter, because the next thing I saw was his fist sending me back down again, slamming hard into my cheekbone. I yelped, and then followed my instincts: I fell on my back and I *stayed* on my back.

Irish ran up behind Brent and threw him in an armlock, pulling him back and shouting, "Dude, dude, that's enough, okay? That's enough!" Brent tried to break free for a second, his eyes never leaving me, and then stopped struggling and stepped back. Irish let go of him, pushed him back a bit, and then walked over to where I was splattered out on the curb.

"You okay?" he asked nonchalantly, towering over me.

"Yeah, I think," I croaked. Then, motioning towards Brent, "Jesus, that wasn't cool, man."

"Yeah, well, neither were you," Brent growled, shaking his head.

"What? There's no reason to hit m —"

"I'm going to agree with him on this one, Sam," said Irish in his normal monotone.

I grasped for words, and finally came up with ". . . What?!"

"I mean . . . look." He sighed, flicking his butt into the gutter. "You've spent the last two months pining over this girl. You sound like Vincent Price in an old Peter Lorre movie. All you think or talk about seems to be *Melissa*. But we dealt with it, right? We figure, you really like this girl. We'll give her a chance." He paused a bit, and continued. "Then, you start spending all your time with her. And don't give us any of that bullshit, you've been spending *all* your time with her. We get more and more pissed. And then you get hurt, and all you can do is knock us around for saying the wrong things."

"I, I mean," I mumbled, "I didn't —"

"No, of course you didn't. Man, we've fucking *missed* you the past couple of months. Do you get that? *We miss your company*. If you haven't noticed, we're your friends. And when this girl, this thing you're so obsessed with, becomes something you can't have, you think we're happy about it? No, we're upset, because we know how much she means to you. And what do you do? You scream at us. Us, who you've been neglecting and putting aside and who've just wanted to spend some fucking time with you. I think we've had about enough."

He finished, and just stared at me in his same way. It was amazing: Irish had just said one of the most eloquent, personal things I'd ever heard, and the boy had hardly even raised an eyebrow.

He was right. They were right. I'd neglected them for her.

But how the fuck was I supposed to know?

175

Pang.

"How the *fuck* was I supposed to know?!" I screamed, jumping to my feet. I was hunched over, leading with my head, my fists thrown behind me like those of a child throwing a tantrum. "How was I supposed to know how hurt and lonely you guys felt without me when *you never fucking tell me*?! I might've done things a little differently if you two had said a word to me about it!" I jabbed a finger accusatorily at Brent, then Irish. "But no! We don't talk about feelings in this friendship. Not until one of the three of us pisses the other two off enough that they have to deliver a self-righteous sermon about it. Well, you know what? Fuck you two! If you want me to take your feelings into consideration, next time you'll let on that you *have them*."

Brent shifted from one foot to the other. Irish opened and closed his mouth like a fish on land, trying in vain to find the right words again. Finally, after a few seconds of silence, he said, "I mean . . . we didn't want to upset you."

"By telling me you miss me? Explain!"

Brent shrugged. "You're in love with the girl, Sam. The last time we tried to bring it up was when we talked about you going straightedge, and you seemed angry as all hell about it."

I wrapped my arms around myself as tightly as I could. They had a point. When they did try to communicate with me, I'd lashed out at them.

"Well, I guess some apologies are owed on both sides, then," I finally muttered.

"Apparently," said Irish.

"I'm sorry I've been neglecting you guys for her, which I never meant to do, and I'm sorry I lashed out at you for trying to tell me I was being a jerk."

"We're sorry we didn't tell you we were angry. We'll try to communicate our feelings to you more often in the future."

"Okay."

"Okay."

We sat back down on the stoop and Brent had another cigarette.

"Well, then, today's gonna be interesting," I moaned. "First, my good friend beats me to hell, then I have to go confront the girl I love."

Brent smirked. "Solid. When are we going over?"

My eyes went up and went wide.

"Um . . . *we?*"

chapter 23
South of Heaven

▷

"You guys really don't have to do this," I muttered as we approached her building.

"Sure we do, man," said Brent, smiling. "We're your friends. We're here to back you up."

Irish chuckled. *Back me up, nothing,* I thought. *You guys just wanted to come along.*

"I'm serious, though," I said, not trying to sound annoyed or angry or anything resembling such. "If you have better things to do —"

"We don't," said Irish. "Chill, man. We aren't coming up with you or anything."

I tried to hide my relief. For a while, I thought their plan was to follow me all the way up. Maybe they *were* just being my backup buddies.

When we got to the door, they both stopped in their tracks. Brent patted me on the shoulder and said, "Go get 'em, dude."

I announced myself to the doorman at her building, who called up and told her I was here. After a short pause, he beckoned with his thumb like a hitchhiker towards the elevator. I walked over to the elevator, perfectly stationed at the lobby (I really did *not* want to wait for elevators right now), and hopped in, pressing the FLOOR 15 button and taking deep breaths. Last time I came to see her, I really had no idea what I was going to say to her. Now I knew *exactly* what I was going to say to her.

The elevator opened and I timidly stepped up to her door. One more deep breath. Think about you and her. Think about her head on your chest, her hand tapping out your pulse on your leg. But most of all, think about you.

My fist went up and I knocked.

My knock . . . damn, my knock sounded, I dunno, *severe*.

How can a knock sound severe? That made no sense.

Well, I guess it could.

But I didn't even knock that hard.

Well, maybe —

The door opened, and there she was, in a turtleneck sweater and jeans. They were almost like work clothes. They advertised seriousness and serenity, with no fun attached.

But then there was her face, which nearly set me off. Cynicism and disappointment were the first things I recognized in that face, but there were splashes of a few others: disapproval, sympathy, and a wee bit of condescension. How could she look at me like that? Why was this all my fault? Why couldn't —

I stopped my train of thought where it stood. *Keep your head about you. Don't let anger fuck this all up.*

"Hi," she muttered.

"Hi," I said, with as much monotone confidence as I could muster. Really, it felt like my nerves were hooked up to jumper cables; my teeth were almost chattering. "Can I come in?"

"Yeah, come on in." She opened the door wider and ushered me inside. I immediately walked to her room, ignoring everything on either side of me. I heard her following behind me at a leisurely pace. Finally, we both reached her room, and I heard her slam the door behind me, and then sit down on her bed. I turned to face her, crossing my arms in front of me and keeping my gaze towards something, anything, on the carpet.

"So," she said, "let's talk."

"Yeah, let's."

She sighed with emphasis, I suppose to make me feel bad. It worked. A little.

"Anything you'd like to say to me?" she asked.

I took a deep breath, and went for it. "I'm sorry. I'm really, really, *really* sorry for how I acted Saturday night. There were all sorts of emotions pent up inside of me, and I let them all gush out. If that wasn't bad enough, I did it in the worst way possible. It was truly unacceptable, and I hope you can forgive me for it. I owe you more apologies than I can even try to give."

She nodded really slowly, and managed to murmur, "Okay. Apology accepted."

"Good," I said, catching up to her immediately. "Now I want you to apologize to me."

". . . What?"

"I want you to apologize to me for treating me the way you did with your friends."

Her eyes went wide. "Excuse me?!"

"You heard me."

She stood and shook her head. "Why . . . why should I apologize to you? I didn't do anything to you! I acted normal, I, I was comfortable and at ease and everything was perfect, and then all of a sudden you blow up like a fucking firecracker and I don't know what happened and now *you're* asking *me* to apologize?"

"Please."

"The hell I will!"

Rage swelled up suddenly inside of me, and for the first time I could ever remember, I wanted to hit the girl I was dating. *Suppress it. This is not a Pantera song. Regroup, rethink, and try it again.*

I cleared my throat and said softly, "Can I ask you some more questions, then?"

"I'm all ears."

I thought for a second, and then looked her straight in the eyes. "You just said you were comfortable and normal and at ease on Saturday night. Do you mean that?"

She nodded, arms folded in front of her chest in anger.

I rolled the next question around in my head before I opened my mouth. "Then what have you been with me?"

"What . . . what's that supposed to mean?" She seemed less angry now, and suddenly more concerned.

"Melissa," I said, and here my throat twisted up and my eyes burned, "Melissa, whoever you were Saturday night was not the girl I fell in love with." And the minute the word came out of my mouth, a big fat tear rolled down my cheek, because I knew it was true. I loved her. I loved her so much. "And now I don't know who you are anymore, and that scares the hell out of me. So, please, just tell me: If you were completely comfortable on Saturday, how have you felt when you've been with me these past couple of months? Because I'd really like to know who I'm dating."

By then, tears had formed two perfect lines down both of our cheeks. I stood there, waiting for an answer while Melissa quivered and shook. Finally, she sat slowly down on her bed and made a noise, a little high-pitched noise in the back of her throat.

"You okay?" I asked.

"I don't know what I'm doing," she whispered, playing with her hands, which sat in her lap. "I don't know. I mean, on the one hand, I care about you —" Her eyes shot up to mine and she began sobbing as she talked. "I care about you so much, Sam, I love you so, so much, don't ever think that I don't, I'm so sorry —"

"Shhh. Melissa," I said. "I know. Keep going."

She looked back to her hands and gulped. "I care about you so much . . . but I . . . it's like, you're my escape from my life. I mean, I love being with you, I love how passionate and sweet you are, because . . . *because* you were like no one I knew. You're different and wonderful and sweet, but you're . . . it's almost like you're not real." She looked back into my eyes and smiled pathetically. "Does that make any sense?"

I nodded and smiled back. "Yeah, I get it."

"Is . . . that how you feel about me?"

I sighed. "Sort of. You were an escape for me, too, Melissa, but . . . I think it was the opposite, actually. I think that I couldn't quite be myself with my friends . . . like I was scared of them labeling me as weak, or, or something . . . but with you, I could be whoever I was, and that was okay." She grimaced; I could tell it wasn't the answer she'd wanted. "I guess that your fantasy didn't line up right with my reality, huh?"

She nodded slowly. "We fell apart a bit, didn't we?"

"Yeah, we did," I said, pinching the bridge of my nose. "I really, really care about you, Melissa. But in the end, I need to be me, and you need to be you. I hardly know who I really am, but what I know I like. And I need that. And if who I am and who you are clash like that . . . y'know?"

Another slow, sad nod.

And another slow, sad breath from me. "Right. I better go, then."

"Sam?"

I looked at her and, Christ, it broke my heart. She had this pleading look on her face, and was just . . . so alone. So deconstructed.

"What's . . . what's going to happen? With us, I mean," she sniffled.

I sat down on the bed beside her and kissed her. Just once, warmly, on the lips, brushing my hand along her cheek.

I looked at her and smiled a little, despite my urge to just burst into tears and start blubbering. "How about I go home, and we think for a while . . . and we'll see what happens?"

She stared blankly at me for a second and then nodded, very slowly. A tiny shred of a smile crept across her face. "Okay," she said.

I leaned in and gave her a kiss, a soft one, on her forehead. "Good-bye, Melissa," I said, standing slowly.

"Good-bye."

I walked slowly to the door, let myself out, and then waited for the elevator. When it got there after what seemed to be forever, I walked in and waited. And right as the door started to close, I noticed her door open a tiny bit, and her face poke out.

Then the doors clicked shut, and I descended.

▷

When I exited the building, I saw Irish and Brent dutifully waiting at the corner and having a smoke. When they saw me, Brent put up one hand in greeting.

"How'd it go?" he said.

I smiled, gave him a slow nod. "It went okay. I think it went okay."

He grinned. Full-out grinned. He looked like the goddam Joker. Irish smiled a little and gave me a slap on the back. "Kudos, buddy-pal," he said. "Celebratory smoke?"

I reached for the cigarette, and then, at the last minute, froze. "Y'know what? No, thanks," I said, lowering my hand.

One of his red eyebrows went up. "No one's stopping you . . ."

I shrugged. "Those things taste gross. Fuck it, I say. A month of not smoking has thrown me off."

Brent gave me a worried look. "That mean we have to stop smoking?"

"Nope!" I chirped.

The grin returned. "Solid. That mean you're giving up drugs and booze, too?"

"Whoa, now," I snorted, "I didn't say that!"

We all laughed. Slowly, we turned and walked towards our school. And I felt a pang. Not a bad one, no, quite the opposite. I felt one of those, those warm pangs, those deep blinding feelings in your chest, where a bit of a lump comes to your throat and a bit of you wants to just up and dance, and you're so fucking happy. I wanted to hug those guys right then, and tell 'em how great they were. But I skipped the hugging.

"You guys are great, y'know that?" I said, smiling. "I'm lucky to have you two."

Irish and Brent glanced at each other, and then returned my warm smile, showing me they understood.

"Pussy."

"Bitch."

"Oh, to hell with it!" I yelled, throwing my arms in the air. "I'm getting new friends!"

Irish shook his head. "Oh, Conan. You crazy bastard."

Brent nodded, smirking a little with a cigarette sticking out of the corner of his mouth. "You know that you love us."

So we just walked, commenting on each others' mothers, and school, and me all the while with a tune on my lips. I felt . . . I felt like me. It wasn't necessarily a good feeling or a bad feeling, but it felt incredibly comforting, like the first night in your own bed after a summer of vacationing and camp. I missed her, and I loved them, and I felt like me, and I realized right then that I hadn't been me for a while. It felt comfortable, and old, and safe.

Right then, right there, everything was perfect.

Well, almost perfect.

A little Judas Priest would've made it *really* perfect.

"You've got another thing coming, duhn-dunna, you've got another thing coming . . ."

☐